The Journey Home

The Journey Home

Marigold Fields

Writers Club Press
San Jose New York Lincoln Shanghai

The Journey Home

Writers Club Press
an imprint of iUniverse.com, Inc.

For information address:
iUniverse.com, Inc.
5220 S 16th, Ste. 200
Lincoln, NE 68512
www.iuniverse.com

ISBN: 0-595-14878-6

Printed in the United States of America

I dedicate this novel to my mother, Marie, who has all of the perseverance of "Rosie" and who walks God's path every day.

Epigraph

"A QUEST FOR THE SOUL"
BY PERRY COURTLAND KENNEDY

I planned upon the familiar path,
    There was no choice to make.
But life had other intentions for me,
    My strength I could not forsake.

In truth, I was forced to digress to a
    much more difficult trail.
One of trying times and uncertainty,
    Of perilous detail.

But as I encountered each enormous
    boulder mercilessly blocking my way,
I did not despair nor from this lane
    stray, but, instead, with deepest faith,
    Learned to roll every obstacle away.

Hindsight offered a different perspective,
    As now reality had shown
That although those boulders once
    seemed large, They were actually
    only stepping stones.

It's not the length of the journey that
    mattered. It's how I arrived at the end.
It's not always where I'd want to leave
    off. It's how I'd need to begin.

I'm not only talking about a change of
    heart, For the better or for the health.
But also a primary course for personal
    growth,
And that I simply believed in myself.

This was not cause for independence,
    Nor my will or desire to roam.
This was a journey back to a place I'll
    never forget, Yes, this was "the
    journey home!"

Contents

Acknowledgements

I would like to thank all of my family members for their cooperation as they were often "cornered" in to listening to my novel aloud so they could render their opinions afterwards. May God bless Stanley, Perry, Samuel, Becky, Lori, and most of all, my parents, Clyde and Marie.

1

The Retreat

The lane appeared longer than before. The trees were towering above in a dense cluster as if to provide a dome protecting the overgrown landscape they surrounded. Yet, despite the environmental changes and the shift in the geographical landscapes, she recognized it. In fact, as she walked slowly proceeding with caution, she tread with anticipation, holding her heart, clutching the very life force that beckoned her back to this place. Like a child, approaching a wrapped gift, she continued to walk with a fervor—a goal in mind—drawn to the center area barricaded by the stick figures of the trees. The wind whirled around her causing her sight to falter, as she had to strain her eyes to see her destiny. On each side of her, acting as her support, were her two grandsons, who were walking slower than usual, afraid to leave her side.

Not realizing why the journey in the first place, each boy did not have the same emphatic step that his grandmother had. Court the elder grandson was a little taller than his grandmother and he held her elbow with one hand as his other hand awkwardly grasped a shovel that his grandmother had urgently bade him to carry with them on their journey. Court was quiet. His placid glances every now and then towards his grandmother mirrored his concern, not only for her physical effort in her journey, but also for her mental reaction to the end of the journey. Contrasting his brother's serious determined gait, was the carefree jaunty walk of Cliff, the younger brother, who at the age of seven likened the trip to a search for a picnic or a play area. He would wound his fingers around his grandmother's other hand until something like a dazzling rock or small creature of nature would catch his attention. He would then

3

dash off, only leaving his grandmother's side momentarily, to investigate. When he thought his exploration final, he would resume his "guard" by his grandmother's side. He held a bucket as his contribution to the trip and often, some things like weeds, flowers, and rocks would find their way in to the bucket during the walk. Court glared at his little brother's antics and careless handling of the bucket he carried. He never could understand how Cliff could act so nonchalant about this long awaited journey. Sometimes he wondered how this little "tree monkey" having arms and legs always moving in every direction, could actually be blood kin to him. Court's opinion was that when he, himself, was seven years old (which was eight years ago), he certainly didn't act in any way resembling Cliff's mannerisms. Noting that the two did have blond hair and very vivid blue eyes fringed by long lashes and distinguished eyebrows, Court decided that the similarities stopped with the physical appearances and in no way did the genes of brotherhood dig any deeper than the skin's outer shell.

However, he was taught from a very young age by his grandmother that what lies in one's inner core—one's very heart is the essential of one's being. Court further decided, now, as he was walking, that his "inner core" and Cliff's "inner core" certainly were not made of the same stuff! Somehow as if to read his mind as he trod along, his grandmother spoke in small breaths, "I could not make this journey without you two boys by my side. I cannot wait to show you what I have been wanting to show you for a very long time. Both of you are such a big help to me and you cannot imagine how grateful I am." Yes, it was always his grandmother's way to intuitively know the right thing to say at the right time. He was not unmistakable in his judgment of her and her ability to unite people for a common goal. She could fill one's "inner core" with the search for goodness as he knew without a doubt his grandmother's inner core was full of a loving, caring spirit and reverence for God. The good Lord knows, he and his brother were raised on the teachings of the Bible and The Golden Rule not only as truths spoken from his grandmother, but also as examples of the very life she lived.

And this very life of hers, at this very moment was so determined on this journey; at least she was bent on travelling this path to something he did not have an accurate understanding of, something only she could understand. Out of respect and love for her, he and his brother agreed to accompany her. It was as if they were enabling her to fulfill a lifetime wish. He remembered how he used to run and ride bikes with his grandmother. She would engage in some type of philosophical talk with him no matter what the activity and she never neglected to make him feel important—worthy no matter what the circumstance. She had a way about her to light a fire within each individual she encountered, leaving that person feeling aglow with wondrous self-esteem and opportunities to conquer. Her positive encouragement was always given sincerely, as if there was no other way to communicate with anyone. Court would often evaluate how someone could genuinely be so happy when faced with the many obstacles his grandmother faced. It wasn't until the past few years that he finally discovered the source of her optimism—her faith in God. She knew to always include God in her sorrows and her joys! She didn't just remember Him when the bad times occurred. When Court reflected on her secret joy, he smiled to himself, because it was only a natural habit of his grandmother to behave this way. It was her constitution of life. Wishing he could be as confident as she, he would often contemplate her advice concerning the ordeals of "growing up" and he would try, no matter how "outdated" he considered her ways to be, to still give her advice some concern. He never let her down which is why he was escorting her today. She wasn't as nimble as she had been in earlier years, but she did walk today with a steady step of energy that pulled her as if a magnet were at the end of this path. He knew her legs were ailing her by now, yet she mentioned no words of complaint. He admired her selflessness. Her walk symbolized her travel throughout her life, really—one of determination and courage with a definite direction. If only he knew his direction! Boy! He would feel so lucky!

As the lane broadened into a clearing and the trees were not nearly so clumped together, she pointed to a building that was seen amid wispy weeds. Cliff ran ahead to explore the "fort" he later used as a reference for what was an abandoned house. Court was relieved to see something other than bushes and pine trees. He watched Cliff bound past the live oak trees that must have been around for the last one hundred years at least. His grandmother's pace slowed, as she appeared to take baby steps to the entrance of the building. The house had been neglected for some time as telltale signs of no paint and wobbly hanging shutters slapped the face of the house whenever the wind blew. The front cement porch appeared to hold up the rest of the house with its splendid round columns. Court looked at the wide front porch and he could imagine this place a refuge on a hot summer day as one could lean against the cool cement columns, or rock in a rocking chair or porch swing at night and listen to the sounds of the crickets and frogs. The front porch gave ample room for several people to recline or sit and view the countryside which was now covered with honeysuckle vines and thickets of bushes and trees. Still, if one erased the dense forestry, one could visualize the rolling hills and pastures that once surrounded this two-story country home.

He held steadily onto his grandmother as she carefully moved from one step to another up the front porch. Looking at her, he saw her eyes glisten with tears. He decided not to inquire why the tears because he felt he would intrude upon her emotions. The silent tour was broken by Cliff's racing from room to room, yelling, "Hey Rie, this place is neat! The windows are so low I can climb out of them."

She was brought out of her trance with his comment, as she replied, "Please be careful, Cliff. This house is very old and I'm not too sure what shape it is in now." Court could tell that as she entered the building, she appeared to recall a vision of each room. He knew her memories were temporarily calling her to a previous time and he again, silently walked behind her, letting her have open space to retreat into her mind of her earlier life as each room must certainly have brought forth recollections. Even though he was looking at an empty ruined building, he was sure his view in no way compared to the view of a living active household his grandmother must be witnessing. He watched her facial expressions change as she visited one room after another. Throughout the entire tour, she still remained teary-eyed and rather quiet. She didn't announce each room as he thought she might. She acted as if she were alone on this portion of her journey. It was when she finally maneuvered herself again to the front porch that she spoke. "I have been gone too long. This was once a beautiful place. So many memories here. So much time has passed."

Court remembered hearing about his grandmother's home place when he was quite young. She would be so detailed in her imagery of pasture landscapes, cedar tree-lined dirt lane, white two-story country house with green shutters and front sprawling porch with large round columns. He tried to compare her description to what reality was now showing him. He had trouble making the connection entirely. He knew it wasn't the building itself that must have beckoned his grandmother. What was here? Surely she knew that homes deteriorate with age if not taken care of properly. There was absolutely "no taking care of" here. If this was the reason for the trip, he was rather disappointed. Still he did not reveal his confusion or disappointment to his grandmother. She never appeared displeased whenever he would show his conquests, dreams, or awards, no matter how trivial they must have seemed to someone with age and experience.

By this time, Cliff was searching about the "grounds" for obviously more content for his bucket. He certainly wasn't disappointed. This was the type of setting for his inventive play that he enjoyed. Cliff was very imaginative and right now, Court could guess that Cliff had captured either Indians or cow rustlers around the back of the house deciding upon their torture or release. Cliff didn't need other kids for interactive play, although he never turned down an interested audience who would like to join him. He was often satisfied acting out the westerns he and Gramps watched together. Gramps and Cliff had a definite bond with each other. They reveled in teasing and playing jokes on others. Court would amuse himself thinking of their "Huckleberry Finn and Tom Sawyer" skits. Gramps was awaiting them at home as Court now pictured him on the back porch of their home overlooking the land for gardening plans. Gramps knew Rie's mission and he assured her he would wait patiently for her return. Gramps also knew that Court was quite mature for his fifteen years and he would protect Rie and Cliff. Court welcomed the assurance of his grandfather's trust and belief. He also knew his parents, while away temporarily on an educational trip, would also be proud of him. Being the eldest grandchild, he had always proven himself responsible and loyal.

At this moment, however, he was fumbling with what specific responsibility was his? Was it to now take Rie back home since she just toured her childhood home? He waited for a sign from his grandmother. She was standing on the west side of the porch with her arms crossed, hugging her shoulders. She was scanning the landscape for a recognizable landmark. What did she still want to see? As far as Court could see, this building was the only landmark worth investigating and it wasn't what he anticipated. He pretty much considered the trip futile as he leaned against the shovel trying to imagine what would keep his grandmother lingering here.

Her eyes seared through the massive tree range to a lower lying area where the plateau of the grounds around the house appeared to dip. Court marveled at Virginia weather. The winds of March ushered them down the lane to the house, but in just a few hours, the warm sunshine of May now appeared to shine upon them from the porch. Spring had not begun to awaken the sleeping forest, as the trees were undressed, making a better view of the area. The nakedness of the forest helped Rie locate exactly where she needed to go. "Would you boys like to walk with me to the creek? I want to see if the flat rocks are still there!"

Before Court could utter a response, Cliff was already helping his grandmother off the porch and down toward the "dip" in the earth. Court hoisted himself up and picked up the shovel to follow. The "farm" must have been quite pretty in its day. He was reminded of Rie's careful description of every floral and fauna found here along with the location of these two hundred and sixty acres bordering the Appomattox River. Not all of the acreage had always been forestry. Rie would never leave out the acres of cotton, peanuts, and vegetables, also including the cow and horse pastures, hog pens, barns, wells, chicken houses, and goat pens. Every farm animal imaginable was housed on this property. Rie's stories of the mule, the bull, and the horses would be comic relief for the never-ending detailed descriptions! Cliff would listen to her tell of family pet stories because of his love for animals. Often Rie would add pet noises to her stories, which really amused Cliff. Walking along through the trees, the only noise to be heard was the gurgling of water as they soon approached the creek where the flat rocks were still in existence!

2

The Arrival

Neither Court nor Cliff had been prepared for the sight before them. A moss covered creek bank exposed a fifty-foot wide creek canal. Helter skelter throughout the creek were rocks ranging in size from five feet to ten feet in diameter. Many of these rocks lined the shoreline. Some of the larger trees lowered their branches over the creek borders. Cliff ran to the rocks to lean over and peer at the swift running water. "Be careful! The rocks are slippery and you could fall in! The current is very swift. Cliff, come back to the shore where you will be safe." Rie had a fear of water stemming from viewing a drowning when she was very young and this fear encroached her mind whenever she was near water. Cliff reluctantly obeyed and began looking for smooth rocks for his bucket.

Court had to admit this place was beautiful. He felt as if he were in a sanctuary. He could not only hear the rushing of the water, but also the singing of the birds. One bird in particular caused Rie to look upward to the sky and stop for awhile. "Boys I need to find an oak tree whose roots are near the creek, barged on a large flat rock. When we find it, I will then need your help with the shovel and bucket." Now it seemed as if everyone were involved in a treasure hunt. Court was so mystified by the appalling beauty of this place, he had to interrupt his thoughts, to concentrate on the very tree and rock Rie described. A soft cry that Court mistook for a bird actually came from Rie as she stopped and sat down on a flat rock that was underneath a huge oak tree. She was feeling rather weak and dizzy and Court worried she would faint! "Rie, please rest! Cliff and I will dig up whatever you want us to dig. We'll do the work–please sit calmly where you are. Are you all right?" Just as Court finished his plea, Rie looked upward to the heavens and sighed wearily.

Sixty-five years earlier the same sky looked upon the same rock and creek in an ominous way threatening rain as Carrie Audra Lorin Wright walked farther and farther into the woods towards the creek. She paced herself carefully and watched for low lying limbs as she made her way to the rocks in the creek. Being nine months pregnant made her journey risky and difficult, yet she felt she needed the escape. Her life had been tumultuous this past year. It was here, the only place she could run away from him, the children, the endless chores, her identity, yes, and her present life. Her present life she needed to evaluate. The walking caused the babe inside her move to place pressure on her lower abdomen. She slowly leaned over to sit on the flat rock beneath the large oak tree near the creek. This was not a virginal journey for she had made several trips to the creek before with a different mission–to end her life.

She never had the courage, though, because Carrie Audra was not a selfish person. Once when she thought she had the nerve, she jumped from one rock to another with her eyes closed thinking maybe Fate would help her fall in and drown. She would be gone and there would be an end to the arguments, the affairs, the demeaning position of her status in her married life—her slavery to him. They had even gone so far as to talk of divorce—a topic unspoken by couples who were surviving the Great Depression. The Depression was one thing, surviving his treatment was another. She would take the three girls; he would take the three boys. She would have to go elsewhere to try and do household jobs for a living. The farm would have to be sold. All of these plans were considered. Then, one night, nine months ago, as a consummation of a drunken argument or either a plea on his part to change her mind, another plan was conceived. She became pregnant with their seventh child. She was only thirty-six and she felt a used woman of seventy!

Whenever faced with her dilemmas, she did remember her Christian doctrines. She was raised on the Word of God. She made sure she passed these teachings on to her children. Her religious outlook surpassed all thoughts of suicide. She knew in her heart it was wrong. She also knew that she was a mother moreso than a wife and she loved children. At one time in her life, she did want to become a teacher, but Landon Wright stole her heart at a community dance and her education ended.

Her mother made sure he was a respectable date. He would face a shotgun at the door if ever there were any doubts as to his intentions towards Carrie Audra. Hannah Lorin strongly believed her daughter, a beautiful young fair-skinned girl with coal black waist length braided hair and blue-green eyes was a treasure to have and she made sure Landon treated her this way! Of course, Hannah's influence on the young couple's relationship could not pass the threshold of their marriage and it was then that Landon's façade of being a gentleman was exposed. Each passing anniversary year he emerged in to a man whose thirst for physical love, alcohol, and power was never quenched, at least not by Carrie alone. After she married him, she discovered he had fathered a child by another woman and the baby boy was born just months after Carrie's wedding day. Carrie took the child to raise because his mother did not show any concern for him. Several months later, the fickle mother decided she wanted her baby back and a year later under his mother's care, the baby boy died of pneumonia. Carrie grieved over the little boy because she had cared for him as if he were her own. Landon wasted no time raising a family with Carrie as Carrie had one child and was pregnant with another within two years of their marriage. Landon was rather proud of his ability to sire children easily and he hoped to have many children.

He was Virginia mountain born of Native American ancestry. His grandfather was a full-blooded Cherokee Indian. Landon's family taught him independence at a very young age. Without any parental guidance, Landon had to find himself through various rebellious struggles along the way. Carrie wondered if he ever "found himself." Still she loved him despite his moodiness and reckless behavior. He was stable in the manner of providing for his family as his stubborn streak helped him to rise above adversities to gain a farm with a sharecropper's money and to fight court litigation and auctions to keep his farm. He realized from a young age that he must depend only on himself, as he,too, had been let down by friends and neighbors. He never gave up, no matter what the circumstances. He became a respectable farmer with his determined look of blue steel eyes, chiseled high cheekbones, and a stature that demanded equal treatment as he delivered his word in a forthright manner. He was a strong man, but it was Carrie's strength that kept the farm going. She never seemed to tire of her infinite responsibilities. Life was hard for post-Depression farmers. The earth was the source of their existence, their survival.

Carrie tugged at the moist ground around the flat rock where she sat. She said a prayer as she reposed herself here. God would help her. He always did. She would bring her problems to Him. Somehow, after each time she prayed, she immediately felt relieved, lighter of the heavy burden she had carried. She had associated this time of year, fall, as a time of dying. Mother Earth appeared to be dying around her—leaves falling, crops withering. She looked around and glanced at the bushes near the creek. She couldn't believe what she saw—**ROSES!** Beautiful peach-pink **ROSES!** They appeared to glow amid the earth tone hues of the dreary surroundings. Winter was approaching earlier than usual for the trees had lost their colorful leaves by now. The roses were the only living plants she saw. She was amazed at their endurance during this season. She got enough energy to leave the rock and go pick the wild roses. They were so delicate, yet so strong. The winds had torn the leaves from all other shrubbery, but the perfectly formed petals of the roses were intact. She absorbed their scent. It was wonderful to feel like a beautiful woman again, lost in Nature's beauty. So lost was she for a moment that she did not hear Landon's call. "Carrie! Carrie!" She jumped and answered back. "Down here!"

Back came his call, "Come on! I'm back from the market! Where's supper?"

She had remembered the yeast on the fireplace hearth for the rolls and the lima beans on the wood cook stove. It would not take too long to prepare the chicken to fry. She also remembered to get the turnip greens and salt pork for flavoring. She gathered the picked roses for a bouquet and ambled up the hill from the creek in the direction of the house. Her long skirts swished past the bushes and thickets as she tried to pick up her speed. Her back was unusually sore with a throbbing pain. Perhaps if she were lucky, after the supper cleaning detail, she may have a few minutes to rest before drawing water from the well for the children's baths and lighting the oil lanterns for homework. Thank goodness the two eldest children, Roy and Ellen were a big help with the evening milking of the cows. Landon would feed the hogs because the children feared their stampeding to the troughs. The third child, Wilma, was to feed the chickens. Logan and Sarah were herding the sheep and goats away from the cow pasture. Henry, the youngest child, pulled his wagon with a few sticks of firewood for the stove.

The evening meal went well and Carrie found she was even more tired than she had predicted. At bedtime, she crawled in her bed and smoothed out the many quilts due to the cool evening air. She tossed, trying to get in a comfortable position. She could hear Landon go to his room and close the door. She tried to relax but her nerves were tense. Her back still ached. Soon she felt the ever-familiar pang of contractions and she tried to endure the long night of pain. Early in the morning, she could not endure the suffering any longer and she yelled for Landon. He arose still peeling his eyelids open as he groggily approached her bed.

"What's the matter? I have to get up for the morning milking, which isn't for a little while yet. What is the problem?"

"I need for you to send for Aunt Mary! My time has come. This baby is very strong and has not stopped moving for the last few hours. Please get Aunt Mary quickly! Make sure the children stay out of here and get their chores done." Her chest heaved with that very request. She expelled all of the air she could afford just to tell him what she needed.

Landon put on his jean overalls, flannel shirt, and boots. He would have to send Roy to the nearest neighbor with instructions to get Aunt

Mary. As soon as he completed Carrie's request, he came back to check on her. She drifted from consciousness to semi-consciousness. Landon surveyed Carrie's room. He had been present for four of the six births. For the other two births, he was either in town or in the lower pasture mending the fence. He placed homemade lye soap and cloths out. He made sure a pot of water was on the cook stove for boiling. He was glad he wasn't a woman because he would not want any thing to weaken his body or spirit. He had been sick only a few times in his life and he didn't like the vulnerable state each illness left him. Landon didn't think any person should ever lie in bed longer than the necessary hours for evening sleep. He pushed the ruffled curtains away from the window to see if Roy was successful in getting Aunt Mary, the midwife. Aunt Mary was not related to the family although she was treated as a member of the family. She was a middle-aged heavyset colored woman who had brought all of his children in to the world. Sometimes when she would visit, Carrie would fix her a cup of coffee and any baked dessert that was available. If Carrie knew Aunt Mary's visit ahead of time, she would bake Mary's favorite dessert, pecan pie.

Landon looked over at Carrie's frail state. She was now looking at the ceiling and he could see her lips move, but he couldn't hear a word she said. He fell in love with Carrie the moment he saw her. She had a slender figure and the most beautiful hair he had ever seen. Yet her prized possessions were her blue-green eyes that were so inviting and warm. Her quick smile showed her excitement to be at the dance. He could tell she was from a strict home environment and somehow this knowledge made him want her even more. He had known many women from his teen years on, but none could light a room the way Carrie did. Her skin shone with an ivory alabaster sheen and she walked and talked so gracefully. Her lady-like poise even made him feel a little off guard. He was so used to being the confident one—the one in control! He never would admit it, but Carrie shook his self-control the minute she entered the room. In addition to her beauty, she was graced with wisdom as she attended a college, a school for teachers.

Courting her in the fashion her mother expected restrained Landon terribly. He wanted to bed her when he first met her. He waited; he played the rules. He won her and she was well worth the venture. He was equally happy to know she could have children. One regret was that the children and farm seemed to sap Carrie's strength and energy and he was used to a lively bed companion, so sometimes he did have to seek elsewhere to release his manly spirits. He loved his wife, but a man needed to do whatever was necessary and his need was great. Carrie would have to understand that she could not satisfy his appetite entirely. As he was turning to leave her room, Carrie's water broke and she gasped, "Don't let the babe drown, Landon!" Feeling helpless as to what he should do, he moved clumsily to pull back the covers to make room for the baby.

The next startling noise was Mary's screeching questions as she rushed past him in the room. "Is she all right? How long? Wuz this her time? Hurry, Landon and git yo'self ready to han' me the cloths, water and bowl and basin! Now git!" Mary didn't hesitate to order him around. At a time like this, the fathers always needed direction and she would give just that. She began comforting Carrie immediately. Carrie's breathing was harsh and rapid! When Carrie saw Aunt Mary, she bestowed upon her an expression of gratitude!

Landon waited in the kitchen and poured the water in to the bowl from the kettle. Roy and the other children were curious, but they knew to stay out of the way. Aunt Mary's arrival seemed to hasten the baby's arrival as well, because an infant's first cries to the world were heard throughout the house. October 1935, Rose Marie Wright was born! Her complexion the same as the rose bouquet in Carrie's room. Her eyes the brightest blue as the outdoor sky and her smile as gentle as the lamb that Henry had adopted for a house pet. Holding her, Carrie's worries vanished. God's covenant was true again. He had blessed Carrie with a beautiful little daughter—a new life that would indeed help enrich Carrie's life. Little did Carrie know, but Rose Marie's birth was a reminder that miracles do happen and life is precious! Carrie nursed the baby and placed her in a handmade walnut cradle. She then placed a homemade rag doll beside the babe. Carrie had made a doll out of a flour sack that looked tea-stained and yellow yarn adorned the head and embroidered roses decorated the doll's lace apron. Somehow, she knew to make the doll ahead of time. Of course, she had thought if the baby were a boy, she would keep the doll in her dresser drawer until she had a daughter. A woman's intuition is a wonderful thing and she smiled at Rose Marie before she allowed her exhausted body to rest. Natural childbirth took a toll on her and she felt weaker with each child's birth.

3

The Discovery

Rie was gradually regaining her strength on the rock. She motioned for Court and Cliff to come near. "If I remember correctly, underneath this rock is where we need to search. You must realize that the earth changes a great deal in fifty-three years and I just hope that it is where I buried it. Even more, I hope it is still the same!"

With that bit of news, Court and Cliff began to chip away at the earth around the huge flat rock. Cliff found dozens of fishing worms and Court had to nudge Cliff's shoulder to remind him what their true search was all about. "What does it look like, Rie Rie?" asked Cliff. "Is it a map, a toy, or money?"

"It is a metal tin that has something more valuable than any of these things. It has something that is a part of me–a part of my life."

Cliff couldn't imagine anything living surviving the mud and rocks he was pitching carelessly up in the air. "Hey, watch what you're doing," commanded Court. Court already knew his hair must be a mottled mess of sticks, mud, weeds, and rocks from Cliff's digging and rooting in the ground. Each boy scraped at the perimeter of the rock, alternating digging with the one shovel. Their rapid shoveling slowed down, as they felt tired from the exerting search and still no treasure.

"Rie Rie, Are you sure this is the right spot? We've been digging for about forty minutes and I think we've covered this area pretty well." Court wondered if Rie's reminiscing was somewhat altered a bit.

"No, I feel sure this is the very rock. Le' me have the shovel a minute and I'll dig in the slanted bank here. You boys rest. I feel more energized just having you with me so I can share what I find." With these words, she took the shovel from Court, who was frankly too tired to protest, and she shaved the bank under the rock. Twenty minutes later, the tip of the shovel hit a metal object. Rie was excited, yet scared. Court took the shovel to help dislodge the metal object. He pulled out a metal cooking tin with a top. The outer part had once been decorated, but the years of hibernation underneath the rock and soil had stripped it of its décor. The top was secure and it took Court's remaining strength to pry off the lid to the tin. He couldn't imagine the content, for the tin felt light and when shaken didn't rattle. Upon opening the tin, he noticed a cloth folded and tucked neatly inside. He reached in and pulled out a discolored flour sack rag doll with stringy dark yellow yarn hair and torn and loose threads from an apron still attached with of all things—tiny stitched rosebuds as a border.

Rie clutched the doll to her heart and she wept. She had discovered the very item she came to seek. She ran her fingers over the cloth, yarn, and she lightly touched the stitching. She pressed the doll again to her chest and her mind wandered to a much earlier time.

"Rose Marie Wright! Where did you hide my good cooking tin? You little monkey! Have you been playing with your doll in the kitchen again? " Carrie was heart-warmed at the scene of Rose Marie carrying the cloth doll with her everywhere and placing her in baking dishes for a rest while she would be at her mother's feet in the kitchen as her mother baked.

She was three years old and her tousled cotton white hair would inevitably be covered with some flour or spice since she was always underneath her mother. She never left her mother's side, from her birth to the present day. Even though there was a set of twins born after her birth expanding the Wright family to nine kids, Rose Marie tried never to let anyone part her from her mother. Carrie, in turn, enjoyed Rose Marie's company and while she had many children to tend to, the little three-year-old holding onto her skirts at this moment was her pride and joy.

Rose Marie was truly a joyous wonder. She never gave her mother any trouble except for a few mischievous deeds such as the presently missing cooking tin! Her smile was that of a cherub. Carrie wondered if her prayer by the creek that evening before Rose's birth was answered by an angel being sent from heaven. She did know one thing—her life was ever so much stronger for the Lord and whatever the cause for that, she was grateful.

Trying not to step on Rose Marie's little legs stretched on the kitchen floor, Carrie danced around as she proceeded to open one cupboard after another. "Rosie, where again is my cooking tin? " The next bottom cupboard revealed the tin with candy stored inside. "Now where did you get these cinnamon sticks? I bet from Cousin Jacob on his last visit! Did you think I would never see these?" Carrie laughed at Rosie's perturbed look when Rosie saw her mother discover the candy. "Now please give me some room to finish baking. I have to get lunch ready. Your daddy and the others will be in from the fields soon and the twins will be up from their nap." Rose Marie gave her mother a few inches to move, but that was all. She enjoyed listening to her mother sing while cooking. Her mother was the best cook. She was like a magician in the kitchen. Rosie never saw so much food cover the large oak table in the dining area. She would look at all the dishes of foods and she would sometimes stick her pudgy little finger in some of the foods for her own taste test!

After lunch, she wandered onto the front porch as her mother tended to Jack and Jaclyn, the twins. To feel she had a part of her mother with her wherever she went, she held the rag doll tightly and cuddled it to her chest as if to reassure her doll that she would always keep it with her; somehow she wanted to reassure her doll of the very feelings she yearned, security and love.

4

Memory Lane

As Rie examined the doll, her blue-green eyes were still misty. Cliff and Court encircled her on the rock as they too were studying the doll. Cliff, as usual, was the first to break the silence. "Hey Rie, what is that supposed to be? Is that what we were to find? How come there is no money or toys in that case? I thought there was somethin' real important in there."

She patiently explained, "This doll was my toy. It was given to me by my mother. And yes, this is very important to me. Cliff, do you remember your stuffed toy dog, 'Moonbeam,' that you carried with you everywhere? And Court, do you remember your stuffed toy dog, 'Benji'? Well, this doll is sort of like those cherished toys you each had except that this was made by my mother and it is really all I have left of her. Now, do you see why I had to come and get it, to see if it was still here and take it? It belongs to me and having it and holding it right now makes me feel complete and peaceful."

Court and Cliff really couldn't estimate the value of this find as highly as Rie did, but they both knew it meant something to her and that was good enough for them. Seldom had they ever seen their grandmother spend money on herself or do anything for herself. She sacrificed for her husband, children, and grandchildren. Rie deserved to have something special, and if this doll was all it took to make her happy, then, yes, it was a unique gift worth treasuring. The boys figured it was one of those "heirloom" gifts that older people acted funny over. They knew from their experience at home, the very gifts they were not allowed to touch because they were considered "heirlooms." Each boy did agree that he couldn't understand the need to save such stuff. What in the heck was its use for the time being and the future? Despite their difference in ages and interests, Court and Cliff did see eye to eye on the value of "untouchable" stuff. What's even more confusing is that doll looked as if it had been touched too much!

Being a mind reader again, Rie said with her twinkling eyes and warm smile, "You wouldn't believe how this doll was my buddy throughout my younger years. I can remember some very funny stories about it if you'd like to hear them."

It felt so good to recline on the rocks in the sunshine and since there was no hurry to search for anything else and they did need a rest before the walk back; each grandson willingly nodded to hear some "ol' timey" stories.

"Well, for one thing, when I was almost Cliff's age, I had my chore list increased from feeding the chickens and goats to watching the cows in the pasture." As she told the story her mind revisited the scene of excitement.

The late afternoon sun was sinking fast behind the huge willow trees in the west pasture. Rose Marie and Henry had graduated to "watching the cows." For the most part they didn't mind the task because they could lounge on the soft grass and guess the shapes of the clouds above. Henry was about nine and he had a spindly frame with an apple-shaped head. His ears protruded outwardly and his older siblings always kidded him about going outside on windy days for fear he would become airborne. Henry was a good brother to Rosie and she liked his tender care of animals. He knew how to communicate with the animals. This was a mystifying talent to Rosie. It wasn't anything for him to be found in the barn rubbing liniment to a hurt leg of one of the horses and talking to the horse as if the animal understood every word he said. With pricked ears, the horse would look at Henry and whinny now and then. On another occasion, Rosie remembered Henry soothing a frightened baby lamb from a snorting hog that was loose. He not only held the lamb in the crook of his arm, but he had the monstrous hog walking beside him to the pen. Rosie knew her mama was fearful a stray would wander on the place because she knew Henry would keep it and they had enough animals already.

Perhaps that is why Rosie didn't mind having Henry as her comrade during the cow-watching task. On this particular day, the clouds merged into one giant cloud. The cows were acting peculiar, which, Henry explained, was a sign of a storm to come. "Animals always know, " he said. Rosie never liked thunderstorms and she grabbed her cloth doll for comfort. Henry and Rosie knew they needed to get the cows quickly into the barn. It would be milking time before long anyway. Rosie laid her cloth doll down on the grassy knoll just to assist Henry in herding the cows towards the barn. As Rosie and Henry were surrounding the twenty-five cows, Wilma, at her mother's insistence, was coming upon them to tell them to come closer home.

Wilma was a devious child by nature and when she spied Rosie's doll lying on the ground, she decided to take it and hide it. Wilma was jealous of Rosie. She looked upon Rosie as a spoiled little sister. Wilma felt powerful whenever she made her younger siblings miserable. Her spitefulness was bone deep for not only did she attempt to commiserate Rosie, she would also show talent in lying about her deeds. Landon's favoritism shown towards Wilma was rather apparent as he always accepted her viewpoint. Rosie also noticed Wilma's boundaries were not so strict and severe as hers were.

Wilma knew no boundaries and when she quickly stole the cloth doll, she walked backward, keeping Rosie in her sight. She didn't notice her direction as she passed through a gateway in the bull's pasture. She was oblivious to the fact a bull was behind her. He noticed her and he probably would not have bothered her except for her animated behavior as she was wildly running sideways. He read her actions as an intrusion and threat and in his defense he began snorting and pawing the ground to charge. Wilma shrieked as she saw the bull preparing to charge her way. She ran around the pasture crying and shouting for help. It didn't help either that she was waving the cloth doll madly constantly.

Henry ran to her aid as soon as he could. He stood in the bull's path and Wilma thought he was crazy to stand stone still. She didn't hesitate to run out of the pasture and she flung the doll at Rosie as she sped by. Wilma didn't stop running until she slid in and out of the front screen door and in to the kitchen. In the meantime, Henry stared at the bull and the bull, sensing no movement or threat, moved in another direction with his nose to the ground.

Henry latched the pasture gate and he walked with Rosie to the barn to secure the cows already there. Later they joined the rest of the family in a laugh over Wilma's escapade. This episode only widened the chasm between the relationship between Wilma and Rosie. Rosie was glad to have her doll. When she nestled in bed next to her mother, after prayers, she would press the doll under her chin and sleep peacefully.

5

Bumps In The Road

Rosie slept with her mother until the day her mother died. She never thought of herself as a favorite or special child. She just felt so comfortable with her mother. Her father scared her with his arguing. She would take the cloth doll and hold it over one ear with her hand pressed to another to muffle her father's anger. Her ears were especially sensitive because she suffered a series of earaches at the age of five and her mother would use wax, oil, and warm cloths to try and relieve Rosie's pain. Her inner strength came from her mother.

She would often watch her mother transform from mother to business partner to farm caretaker to arbitrator to whatever responsibilities called her name. Rie now thinks back to some of her mother's battles fought and won. One saving grace action by her mother was the retention of the farm.

"Carrie, ol' man Phillips claims he has ownership to our farm. I'll be damned if I'll let him take this property. All we worked for will be gone. He's challenging our deed—our rights to live here. I have to go to court next Tuesday. He has no authority—that rotten son of a—why I'll wring his neck when I get my hands on 'im."

"No you won't, Landon. That is just what Mr. Phillips would like—another reason to take you to court and then you'd be in jail and lose this place for good, not to mention, well, you know…" She wondered about the importance of the family to him. She stopped short in her speech; now was not the time to rile him even more. He was in a drinking mood. His way to solve predicaments—to see his way clear—was to see his way clear to the end of a bottle. She thanked God the children were out of the way most of the time their father was in this mood. Carrie didn't uphold his behavior, but she didn't want the children to be at odds with him also.

Landon stormed out to the smokehouse, which might as well have been a wine cellar, too. He kept a jug out there and he would be there to nurse his hurt pride. Carrie used this "time alone" to search for the deed and receipt to the property. Mr. Phillips' allegations were those of an ol' miser who owned much of the county and wanted more. Greed was a destructive force. Carrie remembered the many Bible stories telling of greed destroying the people afflicted with such a disease. She felt sorry for anyone who possessed this evil. She, herself, had not one jealous or coveting bone in her body. She tried to teach the children to be the same way. Rose Marie, Ellen, and Henry were understanding the concept well, but Roy and Wilma were having a difficult time grasping the idea. Logan and Sarah were usually quite influenced by Roy and Wilma.

Carrie knew she was doing the best she could as a mother and battling a person's self-made will was the biggest battle of all. To plant seeds of virtue where the soil is stubborn is a never-ceasing battle for her. She also had age against her–not only hers, but the age the children had become. Roy had dared hit her before and Sarah had hit her with a broom.

Carrie disciplined her children without sparing the rod, but some of the devil's ways resisted even physical punishment. She would have to search for different means. Now she had to search for a written notarized record of their ownership of their farm. At one time when most people's word was a sealed deal, Carrie knew to save written records because she knew the infallibility of something written and the fallibility of a person's memory and word. Opening the strongbox, her fingers filed past birth certificates, a marriage license, and various receipts for livestock until her eyes gleamed and she smiled. The deed and receipt of payment were there, yellowed, somewhat wrinkled, but legible and authentic just the same!

Rap! Rap! The judge's gavel hit the platform. The old county courthouse was drafty even though the room was full of farmers, ladies, and a few lawyers. The wooden benches were creaky and quite uncomfortable.

Judge Harper had a sour look on his face as his furrowed eyebrows fused together as one big brow above his gray eyes. His wrinkled face looked weary and he did notice the wall clock several times in the past ten minutes. Mr. Phillips' lawyer called several witnesses to the stand to verify that Landon Wright was acting as a "squatter" on the property in question. Lawyer Gates was interrogating the star witness, Reverend Stokes. Rev. Stokes was used to large audiences and he spoke with a dignified air quite audibly. He supported Mr. Phillips' accusation wholeheartedly testifying under oath that the Wrights were not true owners of their property. Lawyer Gates called no further witnesses because he felt the minister's credibility established his case. He based his summary statement on the fact that no records were held in the courthouse and that the reputable Rev. Stokes even heard the Wrights repeat (to neighbors) how they were lucky to live freely on this land.

Well, no county is too small for corruption and certainly not at that time for Chesterfield County, Virginia. Human error happens, but money prevails over all. At least it did for Rev. Stokes and many other "eye" witnesses used in the case against the Wrights. Phillips' power and influence crossed over the doors of the "sanctified" churchgoers and the situation looked dismal for Landon Wright. He believed in the truth and the document he held in his hands. He was going to make sure the loophole Phillips found would hang Phillips.

When asked to speak in his defense (he was not assisted by a lawyer), Landon spoke of the bill of sale of and transaction that took place the day he purchased the farm. Landon was well aware of the history of the farm, as it was a land grant from the King of England. He knew the prior owners. Landon cautiously went before the judge. He became paranoid because of the massive number of people who believed Phillips.

"Your Honor, I am the rightful owner of the real estate property as I have proof of my Bill of Sales and receipt of the exact monies paid and the exact land description of my property." Landon handed the document to Judge Harper.

"It appears this notarized document is well witnessed and quite authentic. What I would like to know is why this is not recorded in the books properly?" Judge Harper responded mainly to the lawyers present because a legal person would have been responsible for such an action. "I would like to investigate further; however, Mr. Wright has produced the evidence to sufficiently announce him legal owner of said property and I rule in his favor."

Landon felt a surge of relief. His hands were sweaty and his face quite red. He was glad to have the ordeal finished. He was so happy to leave the courtroom; he didn't even acknowledge the look on Phillips' face. What's more, he didn't even acknowledge the look on the people's faces as they stared at Reverend Stokes as well. Carrie met Landon and they rode "home." Home–a place of sacrifice, sweat, worry, and right now, a place of refuge. Probably Landon never realized that the very place that gave him headaches, or reminded him of all the chores he had to do, was the very place he was proud to own. To own something–to have worked hard for something–especially after The Depression–was an accomplishment. It said something about one's character. "Home" reflected a person. It reflected stability and steadfast endurance. Rie associated her mother's wit at saving the home to saving a place for them to return to someday.

Rie knew her trip "home" reflected many reckonings in her life. She held onto her favorite "home" memories–picking daisies and huckleberries with her eldest sister, Ellen. Ellen had soft big brown eyes and she was tender and friendly. In many ways, Rie associated Ellen with her mother. Ellen was carefree. Later when Ellen was old enough to go live and work in town, she would still visit everyone at home and shower them with gifts. Ellen would try to help her mother in any way she could. Whenever Carrie had bleak moments and her health seemed to fail her sometimes, Ellen would come home to help her. Rie especially remembered the times Ellen would carry her, Rie, on her hip when Carrie no longer could. Yes, one of Rie's rays of sunshine in her childhood, other than her mother, was her sister, Ellen.

Feeling the rays of sunshine made Rie feel warm and content. She looked over at the grandsons who, at one time, had been intently listening to her stories and she smiled as she noticed each boy was napping on the rock by the creek. Rie felt she received her strength from the sunshine. She loved the way the streaks of sunshine glistened through the trees and showed the youthful looks of the boys. Each boy was still so naive to the ways of the world. Where do the simple joys of childhood go? Why are they lost over the generations? Rie reflected upon the Biblical scripture, " When I was a child, I spake as a child…I thought as a child…" Innocence is a virtue, but it is not a survival characteristic. Rie remembered an awakening time in her life when her innocence was taken from her–stripped away…

"Mama, I need Rosie to help me with the buckets of gravel for the road." Roy was a young man of sixteen and how helpful he thought a five year old girl could be, puzzled Carrie, yet she thought Rosie might enjoy the walk and fresh sunshine from being cooped up in the kitchen with her. Roy grabbed a shovel and few buckets. The gravel pit was close to the river and Roy was going to use the mule and wagon to transport the buckets of gravel. He placed Rosie on the wagon seat and they rode off to the gravel pits.

On the return trip, Roy started playing with Rosie's hair and he began tickling her. About one-fourth of the way home he stopped the mule wagon off the trail and grabbed Rosie harshly. She wondered why his touch changed. She thought he was just "play wrestling" but he was rough and he pulled down her panties and he unzipped his pants. This was not play-wrestling and Rosie blacked out with the pain.

She, not understanding what had happened to her, only realizing the pain, took a long time to reveal this event to her mother. Roy had tried to touch her again and she was able to escape. She associated Roy with pain. She was too young to understand what he had done, but she was old enough to know it was not right. After Carrie found out what had happened, she had Roy sent away to live elsewhere. Not only Rosie but also two of her sisters were grateful as well. It would take Rosie a long, long time to heal mentally from this physical act. In many ways, her innocent childhood had abruptly ended. She needed her doll. She needed her mother. She needed to block out the bad memories.

Rie winced whenever she thought of Roy and the shame and embarrassment and pain he caused. For so many years she thought she must have done something wrong. She felt the blame. She felt soiled. It took most of her life and many hours with a therapist and many prayers to God for her to accept and finally believe it was not her fault at all. Her husband, "Gramps," never blamed Rie and he loved her as she was. Rie's self-concept produced this image of guilt and neglect. Her conception of "men" was not a good one because she had two very poor role models–her father and her eldest brother, Roy. Gramps (in his younger years, "Wayne") proved to her not all men behave this way.

Wayne eyed her the first day she stepped on the bus en route to Henry Clay High School. She was a vision of beauty. Her honey gold hair curled about her oval ivory-skinned face as her blue-green eyes searched for a seat. Even though Wayne had shared a traditional seat with Judy, he vacated it quickly to help this beautiful girl with the sweet smile. She was quite receptive to his knightly manners and in no time, they became a couple not only sitting on the school bus, but sitting on the high school steps, sitting at the movies, and sitting after many dances at the Junior–Senior Prom.

A four-year relationship had bloomed for Wayne, as he was now a graduating senior. To secure his relationship with his steady girl, who made Marilyn Monroe look like a mannequin, he asked Rosie Marie Wright to be his wife. Rosie still had one more year in high school and her father had made it explicitly clear she was to graduate before embarking upon a married life. In her heart she knew her mother would want it this way, too. Her father, as a widower, had mellowed some and she felt he was trying to incorporate some of her mother's wishes in the raising of the last three children.

The 1950's were memorable years of her life. Rose Marie was loving her teen years. She emerged from a cocoon of a fragile little girl to an independent, resourceful young lady. She worked hard on the farm, at school, and at a retail store in town after school. Realizing Rosie had proven herself a responsible young lady, Landon gave his blessing and in June of 1955, Rose Marie Wright became Mrs. Wayne Thomas. God must have given His blessing also, because no two other people were better made for each other than these two young people. Rosie remembered love, loyalty, dedication, and compromise from her mother. She remembered truth and honesty as a basis for her married life. Her mother's teachings were Rosie's foundations for her new life in a new home.

6

One Path's End

Rie only remembered her mother letting her down one time—her mother's death. At the age of twelve, Rosie lost her mother to another world, another home. That day gave no hint, no guess of what was to happen. Rosie gave her mother a hug before going to school and her mother wished her well, as usual. As soon as Rosie skipped out the door, Carrie felt a pang in her abdomen as she leaned over the stove. She never straightened up to walk again after that sharp pain.

Rosie came home to find her mother in bed in a weary state. Dr. Forbes had visited Carrie and he didn't give Landon and the family much hope. She had ruptured an internal organ and she had much internal bleeding. The family needed to say their good-byes; she didn't have much time. Rosie would have gladly given all she owned for more time—time to spend with her mother—more mornings to wake up to her mother's cheery good mornings, more days to hear her mother singing in the kitchen, more evenings for her mother to read books to her, more nights to sleep content beside her mother's side. Of all she had—her mother was her life force. She needed more time to tell her mother—"See, I am here for you. See, I want you to live. See, Mama, I love you! Don't go! I need you!"

The bed coverlet was placed over Carrie's face and Rosie's world went dark. She wanted her mother to take her where she was going. "I can go with you! Please just let me be by your side." Rosie didn't understand her mother being covered. She looked at her father and the doctor. "She can't breathe. Mama needs to breathe. Mama, wake up! It's Rosie, wake up!" Landon placed his arm around Rosie to usher her out of the room, but she ran out on her own. She grabbed her cloth doll and her mother's cooking tin and rushed past everyone out the front door. She ran and ran until she came to the large flat rock under the oak tree by the creek.

She cried and cried and there was no comfort for her grief. Her comfort had gone and so she would never heal from this torture. If her mama were alive, she would be the one holding Rosie, wiping away her tears, rocking her gently, cradling her in her arms until she knew Rosie was all right. There was an ache that hurt so deep Rosie felt as if she were throbbing from the inside of her body to the outside. "My mother never left me before. Why did she leave me now?"

With tear-stained cheeks, swollen lips, and wet hair sticking to her face, Rosie vowed to bury her grief as well. She took the cloth doll and placed it in the cooking tin and then she plugged away at the earth under the rock as if every tear and pawing at the earth would ease the pain she felt. She dug and dug a hole in the moist soil that tragic March day. She placed the tin in the pit and then covered it well. She couldn't withstand the reminder of her mother. The cherished doll only conjured a memory that hurt too deeply. Now it was deeply buried just as her mother would be buried, also.

Mechanically Rosie went through the motion of life after that day. Nothing significant occurred at the funeral or burial. She did see a rare event–her father kissed her mother. "Why now?" Rosie wanted to yell. "What did it matter now?" She saw mourners parade by the casket. Neighbors and friends and enemies as well peered at the open casket. Rosie had placed peach-pink roses in the casket across her mother's chest because she knew her mother loved these flowers. She finally faced the casket to get one last look at her mother. She envisioned her mother sleeping as her mother had done each and every night beside her.

The gnawing pain in Rosie's heart was suffocated temporarily by her refusal to believe that her mother was really gone. Rosie was numb to any emotion except her own disbelief. Days were still numbered squares on the calendar. One day blended in to another. Rosie managed to live, yet she didn't know what was the force causing her to do this. She grieved for her mother her entire life. The pain eventually subsided with the years, but the void was always there.

Feeling that her mother abandoned her, Rosie played the martyr for years. She struggled with the chores, helped the twins, assisted her father in business decisions, went to school, and worked various jobs. Little did she realize in her younger years after her mother's death that it was her mother's teachings, examples, and spirit that enabled Rosie to achieve all she accomplished. Her mother had not abandoned her after all. Her memories of her mother's ways strengthened Rosie. Her mother's departure gave Rosie, unknowingly, the courage to be her own woman. She was no longer a shadow of her mother, no longer a child underfoot, no longer a tug of her mother's skirts; she was her own person.

Who showed her the way? Who revealed to her forgiveness in time of strife, patience in time of anger, compassion in time of sorrow, love in time of hatred, faith in time of worry? Her faith remained. God had not taken her mother from her, but actually embedded her mother in Rosie's daily living. Rosie finally accepted the fact that her mother was alive after all. She lived in Court's perseverance to succeed in school. She lived in Cliff's love for nature. She lived in Rie's three daughters–Sheila's spunkiness, Brianna's business endeavors, and Meg's love for children. Rie had come home to tell her mother, "I forgive you, Mama, for leaving me. Thank you for your strength.

7

The Crossroads

Rie repositioned herself on the rock. She saw the boys squirming and rousing themselves in to a sitting position. Cliff looked about to familiarize himself with his surroundings. He spied a frog hopping through a burrow in the ground. Curiously, Cliff left the rock to follow. Rie allowed him to wander as long as he was in her sight. Resting his elbow on a propped knee, Court yawned lazily. "Sorry, Rie, we didn't mean to fall asleep. I guess we missed your last story."

"That's all right. There's always more story-telling time. I feel my memories may not be very enthralling, but you don't know how much I thought I had forgotten until I came here. Looking around causes me to get in touch with my past. My roots are here. No matter how I wanted to grow up and run from home, I couldn't forget my youth, my beginnings! Court, did you ever think life was a cycle?"

Court reflected on her question. He could sense this was one of those philosophical conversations. "I think that life imitates nature and nature is a cycle of events; at least the seasons tell us this with a birth, growth, death, and rebirth."

"I think you have the right idea. I mean do you believe the cycle has to be physical like nature?"

"I guess the life cycle could be mental."

"Do you mean spiritual?"

"Yes."

"You know I feel as if I have united with my spiritual life cycle. The only thing is that when I was experiencing "a life event" such as birth or growth, I was under the wrong impression as to what I was actually experiencing. I

51

mean as to what I should call it. Nature's life cycle is so obvious. We are fortunate here in Virginia to see the seasons as they change. They are so recognizable. Yet, I feel a person's life cycle is not so easily recognized."

Court looked confused. "But, Rie, each event is related to the one before it and the path of the cycle can only go this way. A death cannot happen unless a birth has occurred."

"I don't mean in that context. I mean that when I was going through a growth period, I may still have been in a birth phase as I was introduced to new feelings. And when I felt as if I were growing, I may have encountered a death phase as if my life were in a stalemate position. I believe we can be dead or stunted to what is happening around us until something happens to trigger or awaken us. This could be considered a rebirth!"

Court could make some sense out of what his grandmother was saying. He didn't doubt she knew what she was talking about because of her age and experience. He could never imagine his grandmother in a stalemate situation. She was alive with passion in every aspect of her life. She had an inner strength like no other person. He fondly reminisced when he would accompany his grandmother on errands and no matter how she physically felt, he had to run to keep up with her pace. When those around her were confined to bed whether they were ill or dying, she was there to encourage their will to get better, to live. Whenever he had a set back at school—a hard test, or a rejection from a schoolmate, it was Rie's uplifting words of faith that lingered when all else dissolved around him. Yes, Rie was a fountain of spiritual energy.

"You know, Court, it was at the time of my life when I was so sure of the answers that I actually was a child with so much more to learn. I believed life's path to be straight and simple: no curves, no bumps, no detours. Little did I know that it is not just the direction in life we take, but what we make of the scenery as we go. I know this sounds so far fetched to you. Perhaps an example of what I am saying is that I believe God instills in us the basis of His Commandments and as we travel life's journey, we are in control of our pace and our direction by the choices we make and the route we decide. Earlier in my life, I perceived my direction as being in Fate's hands and I didn't realize that if I were a victim of circumstance, that with God's help, I could overcome whatever obstacle was in my way. I could choose whatever path I decided to travel. I was so scared many times because I felt alone. My mother was not with me during the darkest moments of my life; neither was she there to share the brightest moments. Without her guidance, I felt my path was a dead end. Sometimes after her death, I felt dead. I remember trudging along a direction I thought was what I should take. I didn't have any faith in myself. When I met your grandfather, for instance, I succumbed to his dominating mother and aunts. I wanted so much to please someone and to be accepted. Well, in my attempt to enable their wants and wishes, I was not fulfilling what my future plans were. It took a long time, but with God's guidance, I broke the hold of submission and I was reborn into a wife and mother that willfully defended herself and her immediate family. I had reached a crossroads in my path to which I had to make the decision, which was best for all concerned. Court, often we struggle as a minority, but with God prevailing, the strength is there and the direction is clear!"

"I had depended so much on my mother that I didn't realize I could depend on me. You know it is when the mother bird leaves the nest that the baby birds attempt to fly; when the parent is distanced farther from the child that the child crawls and learns to walk. I've had some stumbling falls in my life, but I learned from each one. You know, I believe, those stumbling blocks were placed there with a purpose. I didn't know I could get up until I fell."

Court knew what his grandmother was trying to say. If there were no mistakes or blunders, there was no learning or growth. He reflected on his own mishaps. He remembered as a toddler he touched a lit birthday candle and burned his finger. Even to this day, when he has to light candles for power outages or celebrations, he is quite cautious!

"Suffering doesn't weaken the soul; it fortifies it." Rie concluded. "Oh, Court, there are so many wonderful memories I have of my life. There are so many ways I have been blessed. When I married your grandfather and I wanted children, I discovered I couldn't have any children until I underwent three operations. I wanted children so badly I saw past the suffering and I agreed to the surgeries. Just think, you wouldn't be here talking to me if I didn't have the surgeries to have your mother."

"I can remember your mother as a little girl who was so energetic that I was played out just watching her. Her love for language and literature is seen so clearly in your interests. Her love for dogs and horses is so vivid in Cliff's hobbies. And what's even more wonderful, you and Cliff will pass these traits on to your own children one day! Your mother also graduated from the very same college my mother attended. Your mother's career of being a teacher was my mother's dream! Again, life's cycle! No matter the paths, we all come home one way or another."

Cliff interceded their thoughts by chasing a butterfly and not a frog this time. He had the bucket upside down poised in mid air just daring the butterfly to land so he could capture it. Rie and Court laughed at his comical way of "sneaking upon" the butterfly.

"I truly believe if you want something bad enough, and it was meant to be, it will happen. One day your mother was seeking out of a relationship with a boyfriend. She was either bored or frustrated. Whatever the reason, she was not satisfied. She decided to go bike riding on the country road that ran past our house. Upon her return biking trip, she slowed down at the intersection to avoid riding in front of a car carrying two young men. Well, one of those men decided to meet your mother and he later came to our house so we could meet him, also. That man is your daddy! The timing was perfect! I often think that if either of them had been one minute too fast or one minute too slow, the chance of meeting would not have occurred. Their paths have merged as one ever since. I felt blessed my family expanded to include your daddy, S.C. I have felt the same way with your uncles, Robert and Jim."

The entire time Rie talked, she held the cloth doll. Court perceived Rie had been reborn even at the age of sixty-five! He thought if Rie can stumble upon obstacles and still trod onward, so can he. She has been a testimony to him. She has been persecuted by her siblings; she has faced Gramps's heart surgeries, not to mention her own many various surgeries, risked almost losing a daughter to a respiratory illness and still she persevered. Perhaps her acquaintance with suffering made her the selfless compassionate person she is today. Court vowed that whenever he faced crossroads in his life, he would take the road his grandmother would choose.

8

The Winding Trail

Rie and Court were captivated by Cliff"s comical antics as he maneuvered himself to still capture the butterfly. As Rie watched, she couldn't help but ponder at how many times she, herself, tried to capture happiness and chase it only to discover that happiness was not a material object to be sought for a claim or purchase or price. God only knows how she believed as a young child that happiness often came to those families who were fortunate in being secured financially. Perhaps it was watching her mother and father toil for shelter, clothes, and food with body actions of fatigue, stress, and worn looks that made her associate being poor with being unhappy. The wealthy people in the community certainly looked more relaxed and carefree.

She pictured her mother dressed in a blouse and skirt and apron with her hair piled loosely in a bun and her slender hands carrying the water buckets or kneading the bread or mopping the floor. Whatever the chore her mother was involved doing, Rie would momentarily watch her mother's determined effort to work despite the worn look in her eyes, the wrinkled fine lines surrounding her eyes and lips, the aging spots surfacing on her face and hands, and her slow movement from place to place. There were many times Rie wished her mother better health and happiness. She wanted to give her mother the gifts of peace, relaxation, and most of all, happiness! What one doesn't know until later years, Rie reflected! As a young child she did not realize that signs of inner happiness could prevail over the body's physical "deteriorating" looks, so to speak. She needed to have measured her mother's happiness by the eruption of hymns her mother would sing while hanging the clothes on the clothes line or her mother's laughter at the children's attempt to wrap the very few Christmas presents lying under the freshly cut spruce tree. She needed to have been aware of her mother's peaceful expression during her nightly Bible readings or her mother's tears of joy whenever a newborn was christened in the country protestant church. Most of all, Rie was very unaware of the happiness her mother felt when at night, while Rie was asleep, her mother would trace the outline of Rosie's face and wrap her fingers around Rosie's blonde curls.

Carrie had just cut Rosie's hair and she heard the excited laughter of the kids as they were gathering the materials for homemade ice cream. It was a warm Sunday afternoon and she had promised the children that they could have ice cream since it was a Sunday and their activities were limited due to the religious Sabbath day. Carrie and Landon prohibited any games, even card playing, on Sundays, so the children searched for some outlet of fun. Sitting on the ice cream freezer as another person wound the handle to churn the cream was not judged as work, but fun, because everyone knew what the results would be! Each child clamored to sit atop the freezer and each was given a chance to keep it still as Landon and the older boys gripped the handle to turn the freezer. When it was Rosie's turn, everyone laughed because contrary to her attempts at trying to keep her feet stationary with the porch floor and her little butt tight upon the freezer top, she whirled around as much as the freezer handle itself! Rosie fought hard her tears as she considered herself a failure at helping, yet her mother's giggles soon changed her mood and she laughed, too, at the scene she must have caused! The ice cream tasted extra good since each had a hand in preparing the treat.

More family gatherings heard the ring of laughter, too, as one of the most memorable times was always Christmas preparation. Somehow, actually like the tale of the Grinch, no one could stop the mood of happiness and sharing during the Christmas holiday, not even the Depression or the ever present work load or the lack of money. The Wright family made sure that Christmas was the most special time of the year and that each child would always remember its magical atmosphere and spiritual essence.

Winding around the staircase would be greenery intertwined with holly berries that the children would find in the woods. The smell of a Douglas fir or spruce tree would fill the air along with the irresistible aroma exuberating from the kitchen revealing the very dishes being prepared-country smoked ham, candied yams, green beans, buttered rolls, not to mention the many desserts—cakes, pies, and yes, the ever favorite solid ice cream cake. The children needed no reminder of the menu because they memorized each year which foods would grace the table and they would certainly remind Carrie if she left one particular dish off the table.

The kindred feeling of happiness trailed though the senses of each child present, for Carrie never had quite as much volunteer help in the kitchen as she did on Christmas day! This togetherness made Carrie happy and she hung on to every minute of the transient memory of this day each year. She was too wise to actually believe this festive mood would last forever and she was afraid to blink for fear the mood would escape. Cheer hitting everyone at the same time was a rarity, so it was a good thing to enjoy it while it lingered!

The oil lamps were lit which helped reveal the beauty of the green Christmas tree aglow with the handmade decorations that hung balanced on each twig of the tree. The children scaled as in height such as stair steps gathered around the tree to place a souvenir of the year that was personally his or her favorite. Some paper ornaments were made from school and some were made from whatever scraps could be found around the house. Placed with pride upon the tree, the ornaments revealed each child's separate personality. Carrie would just stare at the fully decorated tree and imagine which ornament was made by whom. Even though her children were borne from the same mother and father, each child had distinct characteristics. She only hoped she had woven in each personality a responsibility to look out for each other after her life was extinguished on this earth.

After each present had been opened and the children were engrossed in his or her gift, Carrie read the Story of Christ's birth from the Bible. How she could somehow relate to Mary's happiness at the birth of her son, for Carrie marveled at the birth of each of her children as each accepted a new promise and task that the New Year presented. She felt each child renewed his or her growth with the demands life made each and every year. She said a prayer that her family would remember the One to whom they made their master no matter what life presented or where life took them.

Another family ritual was also to remember those who were less fortunate. Landon would leave behind his stubborn and unruly ways especially on this day for there underneath his gruff ways was a soft spot for children on Christmas. He would take bags of fruit to those children whose parents couldn't afford anything for Christmas. One particular family was the Turners whose father, Ben, drank away the family's savings leaving nothing for presents at the holiday time. Landon made sure the Turner children had gifts just the same. Watching the fire in the fireplace, Carrie rested her head upon the wing back chair, feeling a different warmth spread throughout her body–a warmth of happiness.

The thread of Christmas cheer unraveled each year in the Wright household. Sometimes it would tie itself to others as well. Carrie managed to radiate a feeling of inner peace wherever she went. She found happiness in doing for others. She never once denied a child anything that he or she needed. When gypsies would come upon her threshold, Carrie made sure they left with food. Her generosity was envied by the elder rich ladies of the church. To try and undermine Carrie's good works, these ladies would pick her apart as if to physically scatter her pieces like a puzzle, finding some fault with her. Her good deeds probably puzzled these women for they couldn't imitate her at all, so the only alternative if not to join her was to try and destroy her. Their efforts were futile because Carrie's generosity and sincerity touched so many lives who appreciated her that she was placed in many hearts as a saint who walked the earth. Carrie generated her own happiness, doing for others. Her winding trail influenced many generations of those who knew her. Rosie was a strand of the strong thread that held Carrie's will and constitution. Many of the other children chose to go the way of the frayed endings of the thread. Rie knew she would be a loner traveling the path she took. She never regretted her direction.

9

The Right Of Way

Rie could see in Cliff's merriment her own mischievous ways. There were some errors along the way she did regret, but there were some errors she felt were justified. Of course, she laughed to herself about some of her siblings' rectifying ways, also. One in particular dealt with county government officials who came upon the farm for tax purpose.

A 1939 convertible Ford bumped long the lane to the Wright farmhouse. As soon as the vehicle stopped and the dust cleared, a short bowlegged, bald headed man dressed in a three piece suit and tie, holding his hat in one hand and a ledger and pen in the other, hopped out the car to scurry to the front door of the house. He was followed by a tall, lanky fellow whose slow movements contrasted the shorter man's staccato actions. Rapping loudly on the screen door, the short man addressed himself to Carrie as Mr. Hughie Jones. He whipped out a business card showing the county emblem as he stood proud as a peacock, saying, "Ma'am, we're here to assess your personal property tax. We need to ask you some questions. This here is my associate, Mr. Lloyd Smith." Mr. Smith acted his part in the drama by just tipping his hat and smiling, as in if in relief that he was only there as an associate and not the major speaker!

"Well, you'll hafta go ask my husband. He should be disking the lower fields. Jus' walk by those pecan trees yonder and you'll see open fields near the pastureland. My husband, Landon is the one on the tractor."

"Mighty obliged, Ma'am. We shouldn't be long."

"That's all right. I know he'll be there most of the day."

Mr. Jones and Mr. Smith began the descent among the pecan trees to the open field. As they walked with a swifter gait (for they still had numerous inquiries to do that day), they remembered this plot of land being discussed in court a couple of years ago concerning owner's rights. This was certainly a beautiful farm to try and seize! As if they both were thinking on the same terms, Mr. Jones and Mr. Smith decided to haggle Mr. Wright about his taxes. Scheming was their specialty and they felt their business suits and purpose entitled them to superiority over these farmers. Emerging upon the red Ford tractor and its owner, the two men appeared more like wolves than visitors.

Landon drove the tractor to divide the soft dirt piles in two rows. He looked up at the two figures heading his way. He had to peer from under his straw hat that shielded the sun. He couldn't identify the two men, but he could make out the lines of business suits and that attire usually meant trouble. He knew to be on his guard and he kept on with his chore. Logan and Sarah were directing the mule and plow over a parcel of ground close to Landon's disked area. The fields needed lime before the planting season began. Landon knew he needed to rotate his crops after this season due to the "wearing" of the land.

Mr. Jones and Mr. Smith approached with an enthusiastically heightened interest. "Hi, you must be Mr. Wright," Mr. Jones said as he offered his hand for a handshake.

"Yes, I am. What do you need?" Landon showed his refusal to shake hands by exposing his dirty gloves.

"Well, we are the county tax representatives and we just have to ask you some questions to assess your personal property taxes. We won't take much of your time, Sir."

"I can't afford time, but I'll try to answer your questions jus' the same."

The tax men proceeded with their routine questions and recorded the answers as Landon reported them. During the process, Logan and Sarah had unhitched "Druther" the mule so it could graze and rest for a little bit. The name "Druther" fit so fine because whenever someone put this mule to a task, it "druther" do something else! Sarah worked along side her brother well as she was every bit as strong as he was. Some contended she was stronger. Her frame showed muscular arms, but what didn't show was her stubborn temper. Whenever her mind kicked in gear to lash out at anything, she gave full throttle to her adrenaline and her strength was beyond any measure. Her control of her strength was also beyond any measure. She was basically the only one of his daughters that Landon would allow to do heavy chores outlined for males only.

Spreading the mule's blinders along the ground waiting for further directions from her father, Sarah watched the two county men as they interrogated her father. She decided to walk closer to hear a little of what they were saying. She didn't want to make a spectacle of herself upon her parent's business matters, but she detected something awry concerning the two men. She noticed her father's agitation as he wiped his brow with his bandana and then he kept trying to cut his tractor on to continue his work. She really didn't have to get too near, because the conversation was escalating as it appeared the shorter man was yelling at Landon about some tax law he had neglected and the fine for such a crime would be immense and would surely cause him to sell some of his property or go to jail. Landon looked stunned at the two men as if in disbelief at the accusations they were making. Before he could react physically, Sarah had beaten him to the action. Sailing over to the short man, she grabbed him by his tie and began choking him until the red color of his face drained into a purplish hue. "Ack, Ack, " was all Mr. Jones could say and tall Mr. Smith was so taken by the strange uttering of sound coming from his partner that he decided to translate the language instead of helping his "associate." He was mesmerized that such a "filly" of a girl would and could attack his friend.

Landon was able to finally pull Sarah off Mr. Jones and as if the parody was not complete yet, Druther, the mule, decided to investigate Mr. Smith's presence for no other reason than maybe to check out the smell of cologne of the newcomer. Sensing this ordeal was definitely out of hand and not what he had intended it to be, Mr. Smith "hauled freight" (as Landon later told the story) with short Mr. Jones "eating his dust" all the way.

The escape from the cleared field was a singular venture, but the escape off the property itself was another venture, for the two men in their haste in leaving, forgot the path that led to their car and they diverted through the woods just to be spied by a neighbor who was citing "guvment" men looking for liquor stills. This neighbor was rather intent to defend his interest and sales, so he shot several times in the direction of the fleeing "bluecoats" thinking these were certainly the men who had been searching for his stills. Needless to say, the path cleared by the two men in their flurry was more visible than the paths cleared by Landon and his tractor! Never again had anyone from the county tried to swindle Landon concerning his tax money, at least no one came on his property to do so. Carrie did discipline Sarah for her rudeness, but most of the family seemed glad Sarah took things in her own hands, literally!

There was never an excuse for misbehavior no matter what the intentions were. Carrie and Landon also made sure there was never a place for such misbehavior, either. Rie vividly recalled an incident in the church which again reflected "swaying from the right way" but not actually "swaying in to the hands of the devil." Every Sunday morning, the entire Wright family had an appointment and that was at Hickory Hill Baptist Church a few miles away. Expected behavior in God's House was quite different than expected behavior at home. Being dressed in "city duds" couldn't allow too much deviate behavior as it was. Yet, there was no whispering, talking, gum chewing, giggling, and the list went on. It seemed downright endless to the children. The time spent on the wooden pews also seemed endless. The only delight the children received from this "ordeal" was watching the different flowered hats the women wore or seeing who could swish his or her fan the quickest or counting the times Frank Cole would sigh snoring during the sermon. The distraction had to be sought for without any attention from Carrie or Landon.

On one particular Sunday, during the church service, the children didn't have to look too far for a distraction, for it came to them. After Reverend Willoughby would preach his sermon and before his altar call with the hymn either being "Blest Be the Tie" or "Just As I Am," he would allow testimonies to be given from the members of the congregation. Perhaps Rev. Willoughby thought that such testimonies would be a nice finishing touch to his program and perhaps he thought that his message would have provoked some "confessional" time. Whatever the case, he would smile politely and radiantly over his congregation and ask for testimonies, which for any Catholic visitor, would amount to a dramatic "live" audible confession to all, not just to the priest. But the Baptists had their way of doing things and this was one of the many that divided them from the Catholics!

Now, most people that engaged in this activity would normally have "rehearsed" their speech the night before or maybe given the reverend some inclination as to what was being said. The best speeches though were those impromptu speeches which were filled with the Holy Spirit allowing the words to escape, unrehearsed, to fall on the ears of those present that day, that moment. Well, Lois Mundane felt the "spirit." She addled her full bosomed body to the front of the church and turned searching the faces of the congregation for either sympathy or compassion. She didn't appear to be too stricken with grief for her "misgivings" because she kept smiling brightly with her lips fully painted with the reddest lipstick possible. There most have been plenty of lipstick left over because of the residual smearing of it apparently on her cheeks. She kept giving Rev. Willoughby her full attention until he sat down behind the podium at the pulpit. He suddenly didn't look so confident. He attempted to hide his discomposure by trying to hide himself physically behind the wooden framed podium.

The congregation was silent and even Frank Cole must have stopped snoring because the only sound was the birds heard through the open windows. It was a humid summer Sunday morning and the only relief was the open windows and the hand held paper fans that propagated some advertisement concerning the area funeral homes pictured on one side and Jesus kneeling with little children on the other. Lois decided that she had full attention of her audience as she began to repeat she was a sinful woman and may the congregation and the Lord have mercy on her soul. She swayed as she pulled a handkerchief from a pocket of her suit skirt. As she peeled off her lace gloves, she began to tremble while dabbing her mask of makeup and mascara streaks. Still throughout the display of asking for forgiveness, Lois still didn't get to the "sin" itself and the congregation was even more in suspense as to what demonic deed Lois had committed. Reverend Willoughby didn't offer any support in her situation for he appeared to hide farther behind the altar flowers this time.

Nature has a way of helping those in time of need for a decision and as Lois was looking rather pained but trying to smile, a wasp found her cologne quite attractive. The wasp veered around Lois several times and she pretended not to notice its presence. Her voice faltered some yet she continued with her plea for forgiveness. The Wright children were sitting on the front row–(a place chosen for those late to the service) and little Jack watched the wasp carefully. Lois began to be courageous as she batted the aggravating wasp which now was more invasive as it tried to dip inside her suit jacket and whiz around her ears. "I have sinned brothers and sisters, but I am not alone in my transgression." Her voice gained momentum and volume as she lifted her arms with an upward appeal to the ceiling. Not realizing that this movement caused the wasp to trail inside her collar, she further testified of her adulterous behavior with none other than...Reverend Willoughby! She yelled his name in proclamation and the very instant she did so, the wasp found its target on the top of her bosom.

Shrieking at the top of her lungs, she started to move quickly stomping and crying. The congregation thought that perhaps the release of her offense made her jubilant to the point of physically feeling the Holy Spirit within her body. They viewed this exercise as an "exorcism" of its own. Little Jack Wright knew better for he had watched the wasp during its flight and he wanted to help this lady who was in torture, so he grabbed his fan and began beating on Lois where he speculated the wasp was hiding. Carrie and Landon were astonished at Jack's actions and they quickly grabbed their son before he could do more damage to Mrs. Mundane.

Poor Jack was whisked out of the church so fast; he saw each pew go by as if in a blur. He tried to help a lady in distress and instead he was taken outside and given a whipping he wouldn't forget. The other Wright children were also summoned out of the church; therefore, no one really witnessed the aftermath of Lois's confession of her affair with the minister. Needless to say, there was not an altar call or final hymn that day and the event was resolved with the eventual replacement of the Baptist minister who needed to go on a "leave of absence."

Jack attempted to right a wrong in his own way. His bold action was necessary as seen by the rest of the children. Rie chuckles even now, as she looks back on the day that the church service was quite meaningful as to the absolution of sin and the necessity of retribution. Jack's unforeseen childlike actions certainly added more to the parable of having a child's innocence to entering the kingdom of heaven.

Rie continued to watch Court join Cliff in the butterfly chase. Cliff's increasing determination reminded her of Gramps's determination. In his own way, Gramps, too, decided to right a wrong. She often reflected upon Gramps's influence in her path of life. He was her motivation whenever the hills were too steep or the road impassable. He would forever be her energy and source of willpower. Gramps would encourage Rie when she doubted her direction.

Actually, Gramps was the knight in shining armor who rescued Rie from the turmoil of her life at home on the farm. She surely felt as if she were a damsel in distress penned on the farm by a strict father who oversaw all of her chores and allowed her no leisure time or hobbies. Rie obeyed the ramifications her father had built enclosing her within the walls from society partially because she knew her father was attempting to enforce her mother's values and character and partially because she saw her father aging with only a few of his children there to abide with him. Rie played the part of the diligent daughter, only going to and from school and to her retail job at a store. She knew her father meant to teach her responsibility and she knew from her mother's insistence, the importance of education. Knowing the family's economic situation, she also realized graduating from high school was indeed a feat and thinking of college was but a dream.

Dreams were conjured by others, Rie always believed. She never dreamt of finding a "soul mate" such as Wayne Thomas who would fill the void of belonging in her life that her mother left. Remembering how she looked to her mother for cheer, she also discovered cheer in Wayne. He was full of humor and smiles and oh, all of the positive feelings life had to offer. Wayne knew hard times such as the death of a father when Wayne was only twelve and the need to work from that age on to help his mother and younger sister. Wayne looked beyond the endless days of work and other responsibilities to peer into the silver linings the clouds also offered. He didn't dwell on negative happenings, but instead, he uplifted Rie with further dreams and opportunities. She noticed how popular he was in school because of his sincere sense of humor. He wasn't rich or famous, but he was a unique individual. He was sent to her from her Heavenly Father, who knew from Rie's many prayers that she needed someone. Wayne was the answer. Both Rosie and Wayne were running in the same storm, seeking for a way out when they ran in to each other's arms, finding the solace they both needed.

Yet, arriving in each other's arms was more difficult than Wayne had anticipated. He knew from the moment he saw Rosie climb aboard the school bus steps that she would be "his girl." Wayne worked hard for everything in his life and now he had to work even harder for Rosie. She was willing to be his girl, but her father was having second thoughts. Landon actually had nothing against Wayne himself; it was the thought of losing Rosie. Whenever Wayne would come to "court" Rosie, he was told she was too young to date. When she finally reached the acquired dating age, she could only stay out for an hour. Wayne noticed the difficulty in trying to see Rosie and he still persisted in dating her. Rosie often wondered whether she was the challenge or whether her father was the challenge.

Wayne realized he had to continue to win Mr. Wright's approval. In the meantime, he had to make sure that no one else would try and court Rosie, so he went to school and passed the rumor that Rosie's father stayed on the front porch with a loaded shotgun ready to aim and fire at any prospective date for Rosie. Well, Wayne had the appeal and charm of a good ol' country boy well respected wherever he went, so no one doubted his word. Rosie indeed did not have to worry about any visitors. Wayne had seen to that problem! This maneuvering allowed Wayne time to speak to Mr. Wright. One fall evening, after school, Wayne decided to visit Mr. Wright, to speak his concerns.

The lane leading to the Wright farm was unusually dusty. "C'mon, Wayne," retorted his pal, Andrew. "Couldn't you 'ave waited another time for me to drive you down here? What if ol' man Wright starts shooting when you get out of the car? Even worse, what if he shoots my car?"

"Don't worry, Bughead!" Wayne always had a nickname for everyone. Very seldom did he call people by their real names. "Mr. Wright will remember me and know that Rosie and I have been friends for some time and he knows my friendship means something to Rosie."

"Yeah, well if you mean so much to Rosie, how come you aren't able to take her out on a date yet?" Andy was still jittery as he envisioned his car as the dust covered bullet-holed car he may need to use as an escape car in just a few minutes. It certainly wouldn't be the first time. In fact several times did he have to squeal wheels and drive quickly as Wayne would have one foot on the floorboard of the passenger side and one foot dragging the loose sparse gravel in the lane from Rosie's house. Some days Mr. Wright was in a temperate mood and some days he wasn't. Andy just prayed today Mr. Wright would be in a more compassionate mood.

"I've thought of a different approach," Wayne replied rather annoyed that even Andy didn't have faith in him. "I've decided to tell him how I feel about Rosie and that I am asking for his help, man to man. I figure if

I still let Mr. Wright know he is in control, and that I am asking for his advice concerning Rosie then maybe he will not feel challenged or threatened in any way and he will still receive the respect he deserves. I will also let him know that his expectations for Rosie will be upheld."

Andy was waiting for some type of trick or joke. What was the magic in this plan? Andy knew that he, himself, wasn't the "sharpest tool in the shed," so he just relinquished the idea of analyzing Wayne's tactics and he decided to see the outcome, whatever direction it ran and whatever direction he would have to run also.

As he coasted the car silently up to the front porch area, he nervously kept the key in the ignition and his foot on the gas pedal and the clutch ready to go. Experience had taught him to be ready! He then watched his friend with very little ammo meet the foe! Andy wished him the best. Wayne must love this girl because most guys would have given up after the first encounter with a ruthless man as Mr. Wright.

Wayne mustered up enough strength to walk up to the screen door and knock hard a few times. Mr. Wright was hard of hearing and being resistant to having any type of hearing aids, he resolved to get by with demanding his communicators yell when they would only have to talk. The light was on in the kitchen and Wayne sighed a relief that no one had gone to bed yet. Waking up Mr. Wright would totally ruin his reason for asking to speak to him. After a lengthy time at checking his attire, looking at the front porch, and watching to see if Andy was still in the driveway, Wayne saw the front door finally open.

As Mr. Wright turned on the outside porch light, he squinted his eyes to see who the visitor was. He opened the door and noticing it was only Wayne, he asked, " What do ya want, son? If ya expect to see Rosie, you know my rules concerning a school night. She's upstairs sewing and she probably hasn't opened one of them school books yet." He still talked to Wayne outside on the porch without offering for him to come inside.

"No, sir, I didn't come to see Rosie." Wayne noticed Mr. Wright's furrowed eyebrows knit in confusion. "I came to see you, Sir."

"Well, what in darnation do you have to see me about, boy?"

"I came to talk to you about Rosie." Sensing he'd better go on with his plea before Mr. Wright drew the wrong conclusions, he immediately stated, " I wanted to talk to you about courting her and what you define as rules for such a courtship, sir." There, breathed Wayne. He didn't know whether to shut his eyes or run or yell to Andy to go any way and he would try and catch up with him later on foot or what the heck to do. Part of the admission of what he feared to unleash was now out. It hit the cool damp air just as he thought he saw the cool chill of Mr. Wright's expression. Somehow, though, tonight, the expression was not so chilled.

Landon Wright felt worn from the exhausting day and lately he didn't look forward to retiring for the evening because it only meant he had to look forward to the beginning of another day to continue his routine of living. For each year after Carrie's death, life proved to be more and more meaningless for him. He knew he wasn't the loving husband or supportive father he should have been, but it was so easy to treat Carrie in such a demeaning manner because she didn't protest as he had hoped she would have. Damn her forgiving ways, her tolerance with his affairs, her angelic qualities! When he did have the courage to try and get a reaction from her as to how much she loved him, he often felt he was confessing to a saint instead of angering a mortal woman, his wife! Landon wanted Carrie to get mad at him, to accuse him openly of his lustful behavior, for in doing so, he felt she were claiming him for her own. He never had anyone to make him feel he belonged totally to that person. Carrie's attention to the many children drove Landon further away. He needed her attention entirely and he hated sharing her with any others. His solution to his problem was to seek attention from other women who had time for him. None of the women occupied his soul and heart the way Carrie did though. Carrie's hold on him was everlasting for each night he was still visited by memories of her long black hair, her blue-green eyes, her warm reassuring smile, and the ever graceful way she had of touching all of him when she would just merely brush his hand, or stroke his hair from his forehead.

Landon had just sat down and gotten comfortable in his raggedy wing back chair hoping for more memories of Carrie to help him pass the last conscious moments of the evening when he was roused by the knocking on the door. He knew from the sound of the car outside, the Thomas kid had come to probably try and see Rosie. Landon fought hard to keep Rosie there with him, because even though he had visions of Carrie in the evening, it was Rosie's eyes, face, and sweet nature that kept his vision of Carrie alive during the day!

"What about my rules do you not understand?" Landon demanded. How could anyone not understand the simple rules he laid down concerning dating Rosie, he wondered. She was not to go out unless her youngest sister, Jaclyn, accompanied Rosie and her date, she had to be in by eleven o'clock p.m., and she could not date on school nights. Landon thought he made it perfectly clear to this Thomas boy what the conditions were. Except for a few alterations in which Landon had to always approve the nights in particular Rosie could go out, and that she was never to be in the company of two or more men at the same time without another female in the car while traveling, Landon thought he had more than compromised his daughter's social needs. All of the older children were married and on their own and even though he wasn't as strict with them, he still felt his "conditions" are what is best for Rosie. Eyeing the Thomas boy carefully, he waited to keep up his guard to be ready for a defense. Yet, as he watched the Thomas boy stand there, he was somehow reminded of his endless encounters with Carrie's mother, Hannah, and what he thought back then to be ridiculous measures for dating Carrie. Landon didn't perceive Wayne to be a threat to his daughter in any way, yet he felt it was his dutiful right as a parent to protect his daughter from hurts and harms that seemed to be bestowed more on young ladies than ever by young men. Landon needed to do "what was right" by his daughter because he did fail her mother.

"Mr. Wright, may I come in and talk to you?" Wayne had worked up enough adrenaline to get this far and he wasn't going to be rejected yet. He just couldn't. How many times had he practiced what he was going to say? How many times had he pretended the dresser mirror was Mr. Wright as he talked to it trying to make it see that his feelings for Rosie were more than just casual chaperoned dating or talking to each other at school? How many times had he ridden with Andy on the main road hoping to turn down the lane to Rosie's house, only to become afraid and keep on going? This time he traveled the lane with a mission and a quest. He would fight for Rosie!

Landon cautiously, but unwillingly, moved to the side so Wayne could enter the foyer. Landon turned around and Wayne assumed his cue to follow the elderly man into the family parlor. As Landon settled himself again into the same wing back chair, Wayne looked around for a closer seat to Mr. Wright since he knew of the man's hearing difficulty. Wayne felt as if he had made a major breakthrough just entering Rosie's house. Before, when he would pick up Rosie and her younger sister, Jaclyn, he only made it to their front door. He looked around the parlor to see that it was kept very nicely despite the absence of Mrs. Wright. Rosie had often babbled to Wayne of the many duties her mother had accomplished. Wayne could perceive Rosie's pride in her mother, and at the same time, her longing for her mother. Most of the teens would sometimes appear very critical of their parents and enjoy any absences from either parent. Rosie would only wish her mother were alive so she could relate to her and share with her, daily events or special occasions. Wayne thought of the many unique qualities of Rosie. Her desire to share with him her closeness to her mother added to Rosie's portrayal of a girl who was real and "down to earth." Wayne treasured Rosie's unpretentious nature. Many of the high school girls tried very hard to impress the boys with false personalities. Rosie's sincerity shone through each time. Everyone who knew her respected her and Wayne considered himself a very fortunate guy to have Rosie for his girl. At least that is why this very meeting this very minute–to lay claim on "his girl

Landon studied Wayne as he watched Wayne settle in a nearby chair near a small coffee table. Landon realized the boy must have courage to face him because Landon had deliberately been very cold and harsh towards many of Rosie's friends. He decided with her schedule that she didn't have much time to communicate with others. He contemplated her being further away from him if he did allow her more time to engage in social activities. Landon felt ill at ease just thinking about losing Rosie. It would mean losing Carrie again.

"Ya say you're here to get my rules of courtship what was that, ya said, 'defined'?" Landon asked.

"You see, Mr. Wright, I understand your reasons for making sure Rosie is treated with respect and treated like a lady, and, Sir, I always treat Rosie this way. I wouldn't treat her any other way because, well, because, Sir, I have plans for Rosie and myself." Before Landon could intercede, Wayne decided to keep his ideas flowing and he poured from his heart the next "plan" he intended to state. "I love your daughter, Sir, and I would like your blessings and permission if you see fit to give, Sir, to marry Rosie. You see, I am finishing school this year and I know I am old enough to provide for and support Rosie when I finish school. I already have job offers and, Sir, I work each day after school and also during the summers as it is. I have been supporting my sister and my mother, so I am a very responsible person." Wayne paused because he realized he was dominating the conversation and for a very good reason: he was afraid of Mr. Wright's answer and he felt as long as he was talking he wouldn't hear the "no" that he just felt sure he would hear. He even closed his eyes when he heard Mr. Wright begin to speak.

The only sound for quite a while was the loud ticking of the grandfather clock as Wayne swore each ticking stole a moment of his life while he waited to hear Mr. Wright's answer. Wayne now knew what it must feel like to be an accused criminal facing a judge's decision, or what it felt like to be a terminally ill person awaiting a test result from a doctor, or even what it felt like to be a parent counting the breaths of a newborn babe while he or she slept soundlessly during the night. Wayne's future hung in balance at the long moment and he struggled with the apprehension he felt. He looked finally at Mr. Wright and saw not only weariness, but also, fear. Wayne had never anticipated Mr. Wright ever showing fear, but here in the depths of Mr. Wright's icy blue eyes there were pools of stormy clouds emerging as if a squall were rising and no one could hide from the tormentuous waves to follow.

"Son, I cannot grant permission to marry my daughter at this time." The words tolled like a death bell in Wayne's ears. Landon thought he himself would not be affected by the boy's reaction to the answer, but he found himself again taken back many years ago and he wondered how he would have reacted if Carrie's mother had given him the same answer. He saw Wayne's spirit escape from him as Wayne limply stared at his hands in his lap. The boy's whole body seemed to collapse with the demolishing answer. Landon thought he would feel the victor and he would be safe and live forever now with his daughter to always take care of him. The thought that he relished before now created a distaste in his mouth as he imagined this boy going through life without the one he loved. By the same token, Landon realized that by holding Rosie captive during her life might just cause Rosie to despise her father for years to come. Landon could not endure the thought of losing Rosie's love. Losing someone to another did not have to mean losing that person's love. Also, wasn't this Rosie's future that he was sealing without her feelings considered? Was this the way he often treated Carrie? Didn't he lose her before she was gone from this world? Hadn't Landon learned something the hard way concerning relationships? Why was loving someone so difficult?

Watching Wayne battle with the decision uttered, Landon further added, "I can't allow Rosie to marry now, because she needs to finish school. She has one more year of high school. I need to find out myself your intentions concerning my daughter and I have discovered time is a good way to see the truth. You have my permission to court Rosie for a year and then we will see how the relationship endures this time period and whether you are both ready to make a commitment to be married. But I do have one very strong stipulation and that is that if you marry each other and you do not treat her right or you find you do not love her, she is to come home to me, and you will never see her again. If you break your vow to her in any way and harm her in any way, you will regret knowing me and you will certainly feel my wrath! Do you understand?"

Wayne, awakened by the roar of Mr. Wright's threat, nodded his consent. He didn't feel elated with victory, but he didn't feel depressed with defeat, either. He still had Mr. Wright's consent to date Rosie, hopefully without her younger sister's presence. He was given a grace period to further prove himself to Mr. Wright and he would do just that! "Mr. Wright, you won't be disappointed. You will see my honest intentions for your daughter. I will continue to show my devotion to her. She is my happiness. I earnestly couldn't imagine living without her." Wayne stood as he held out his hand to Landon. Landon arose still with an intense look at Wayne. Landon had learned to judge people not by their outward appearance, but by the way they looked him in the eye. Wayne's responding stare was sincere, Landon could tell. Despite the torture Landon had put the boy through, Wayne maintained his respect for Landon and somehow Landon knew this. Landon perceived Wayne's visit as one of many to come in the future. He never got close to any of his "in-laws" but something told Landon he might just see Wayne in a different light compared to the other daughters' husbands. If Rosie thought he were special, then Landon would resolve to give him a chance. Rosie definitely had an intuitive manner in searching the souls of others. Landon would always hope she would forgive him for his errors and mistreatment of Carrie, and find within her heart, a place for him. As he became older, he became less stubborn in acknowledging his failures and repenting his past wrongdoings. He never knew when the end of his path in life would arrive and he surely wanted to be ready for Heaven's gates. There he would see Carrie, and have another chance to tell her he loved her. There were so many wrongs to correct and he often felt he had so little time.

10

Paving A New Road

Cliff began examining a fallen bird's nest near the huge rafter-like oak tree that appeared to be shielding the creek area from the sun's penetrating glare. The moss flooring of the area gave an impression that it would cushion anything that fell its way, which may have helped the tiny bird's nest, for it was still intact. There was no sign of eggs so hopefully the baby birds had finally emerged to fly away on their own. Cliff was cupping the small nest in the palm of his hand as if he had something to do with its creation. He saw the building materials of the nest as little scraps of nearby construction materials such as twigs, twine, vines, and so on. Court was trying to alarm Cliff that some materials found in the nest might prove to be harmful in the way of spreading a disease. Cliff ignored his older brother's advice and he proceeded to tug at the wound materials as if to try and rip apart the nest. He discovered the weak looking materials were strong when tied together as one and still prying, he had trouble tearing the nest in to sections. Rie watched closely as Cliff attempted to dissect the nest. She couldn't help but think how this nest, a natural creation, was so similar to a family. The mother bird knowing her time, had built the most secure home she could to provide all the necessary structure, shelter, and means of protection for her little ones so they could grow and receive the nourishment they needed to eventually leave their home to carry on the tradition again. She wondered where those baby birds were and where were their parents.

Rie thought of how the mother bird must have spent all of her energy nurturing her family only to prepare them for a life of their own that would not include her. If her life story were depicted on a painted canvas, she would imagine herself as this mother bird who had for some time concentrated on taking care of her children, only to know that someday they would be in flight in different paths all their own. Colors of pastel blues, pinks, and yellows would hint at the births of her three daughters. Sheila and Brianna were both born in the spring and to commemorate their births the backdrop would have hues of soft green meadows, light brown trees with boughs full of spring green leaves and flowering pink and white dogwoods. Megan's summer birth, on the other hand, would be announced with a bright florescent yellow sun, and dark blue iris flowers mingled with orange–yellow sunflowers contrasting a vivid deep meridian blue sky.

Rie let her mind race back to the days of her motherhood when she could breathe in the smells of baby powder, hear the loose beads in the baby rattle, and feel the soft cotton of the little nightgowns that left a tingling feeling when brushed upon her skin. She absorbed the mental scene of the nursery containing stuffed animals scattered about a braided rug on the gleaming hardwood floor and a motionless rocking horse being covered intermittently by white ruffled curtains flowing from the breeze coming through the large window. She saw a painted white chest of drawers and a white dresser with a large framed mirror hung above. A white crib was on the other side of the room running lengthwise from one corner to the other. Peering into the mirror, Rie gasped at the young woman of twenty-one who rested in the rocking chair in the middle of the room. The woman was napping while resting one arm across her protruding belly that was snug even under the maternity top. Her slender legs rested on a nearby ottoman as her shoes had been carelessly tossed about the floor. Her exhaustion was evident from the heavy breathing and the lifeless appearance of the other hand, which dangled limply from her wrist resting on the armchair of the rocker. Peering further, Rie noticed the rosy hue of the woman's cheeks and the glowing honey blonde hair that reflected highlights from the afternoon sunshine casting its warmth into the room. Rie remembered the nursery's silence as it was holding its breath for a momentous event or revelation of a longtime secret.

Breaking the silence was Wayne's hollering that often had a yodeling effect on anyone within earshot. "Hey Moonshine, how did it go today?" he asked while tearing off his work uniform and wiping his face with a kitchen towel instead of the bath towels he was instructed to use. "Did you get to see Dr. Talbot?"

Stretching to avoid the cumbersome leg cramps she noticed she had to endure of late, Rosie lazily glanced at Wayne with one willing eye and replied, "Yeah and boy am I hoping this would be the last examination until the baby arrives. I feel as if I have been kneaded like a piece of dough. Wayne, I don't think I can even move from this rocker!"

"Now that doesn't sound like the little woman who crawled through the bedroom window a couple of weeks ago to unlock the front door! Where's all that burst of energy that's suppos' to happen before the baby comes?"

"I'm afraid it escaped through that very window I had to crawl through. I still have more to do to the nursery and I don't know how I'll get it all done. You're having to work longer shifts lately driving the delivery trucks. I sure hope you will be in the area when I feel the first pain. Really, Wayne, what am I going to do?"

"Ah, rest easy, little liver lips. I'm sure that I'll hear you howl even a few miles away on my route." He then had to dodge the few stuffed toys thrown his way as Rosie attempted to make him realize, even in a teasing way, that she did need him especially since she felt her time was quite near. "Besides, " Wayne retorted, " I asked the boss for fewer hours just temporarily and a very close route until your stay in the hospital is over. Thank goodness it isn't vacation time yet and there are still enough route men available for switching schedules."

"I don't want to be alone. You know there is practically no one on my side of the family to stay with me."

Wayne understood Rosie's predicament. They couldn't depend on his family for help. His father had passed away before Wayne even knew Rosie and Rosie couldn't contend with the domineering manners of Wayne's mother and aunts. About a year after their marriage, they had pretty much severed ties with some of her brothers and sisters. Furthermore, it seems that Mr. Wright became more ornery in his old age and he would allow his sons and daughters to talk and belittle each other whenever they would come to visit him. Most of the couples thrived upon seeing how much they could demean each other and Wayne would feel sick just watching how cruel they would be. Rosie didn't approve of their actions, but she still felt she should visit her father. Wayne decided instead of the regular Sunday visits, they would visit Mr. Wright during the week to avoid the others. This change worked well and Mr. Wright was always a different person around Rosie. He surprisingly would be remiss if for some reason Wayne couldn't make a visit or two because Mr. Wright enjoyed Wayne's jokes and laughter. Mr. Wright would smoke his favorite cigars, sit in his favorite chair, and "chew the fat" with Wayne, letting out chuckles between puffs of the cigar.

Rosie would sit on the sofa gazing at the antique pictures of her mother. She had been separated from her mother for about eight years now and it seemed like an eternity missing her mother's soft voice singing either in the kitchen or in the yard. The voices of her father and Wayne were a million miles away as she crept back in her mind envisioning her mother scurrying from room to room with rags to clean the furniture or a laundry basket of clothes from the clothes line. She could even imagine the aromatic smells of homemade rolls and black-eyed peas and salt pork simmering on the wood stove. The pendulum of the grandfather clock slowly swayed from right to left as it erased one minute after another. It announced a new hour of a new time and Rosie thought about the many years and the many erased minutes from the past. She now had a new life with Wayne, and her mother had not been there to prepare her for being a wife much less being a mother! Somehow, though, she would feel her mother's presence at the singular moments when she felt all alone.

Wayne threw the dirtied kitchen towel in the laundry hamper and he went to get a cold drink from the icebox. Rosie inched herself out of the rocker and grabbed the dust mop to clean the hard wood floor that was exposed around the braided rugs. As she languidly moved around trying not to bend her body for fear she would be stuck in that position, Rosie studied items that were at least waist high. She rearranged the baby items on the dresser and then she refolded the cotton blanket on the crib. She paused as she neared the old wooden walnut baby cradle that was nestled in the corner of the room. She rubbed the worn wood surface that gave way to pits and craters of abuse through the years from either receiving knocks from toys or just being moved from one place to another. Rosie smiled as she patted the corners of the cradle. She remembered that she was the last of the children to occupy this very cradle as the twins lay in another crib built for the two of them.

Rosie had never really acquired anything from the house after her mother's death except for this cradle and a few other small items that were very dear to her. Her older siblings fought over whatever they believed to be of monetary value from her mother's things, but Rosie was quite satisfied with cards bearing her mother's signature, cooking tins tarnished with rust, but used by her mother, and photographs, and any fragments of clothing her mother had once worn. She was quite lucky to also have salvaged a few children's books that her mother would read to her at bedtime. One in particular was *The Secret Garden.*

Rosie remembered she had escaped some wrath from her father for not doing some chore correctly and she would run to her bedroom and leap upon her bed to recline on her stomach. She would then reach underneath the bed to retrieve one of her favorite books *The Secret Garden* and try to read where her mother had left off the night before. Her mother always promoted reading as a gateway to improve oneself. The Wrights' situation as a farming family did by no means give any excuse for any of the children to be illiterate. Carrie was a firm believer in education. She read bedtime stories with vivid expressions trying to entice each child to venture forth with curiosity to read the rest of the book whenever she knew she would not be there to complete it.

With tears in her eyes, Rosie remembered that *The Secret Garden* was the last book she remembered her mother reading aloud to her. She and her mother would dream of the many flowers they would someday have in a secret garden of their own. Her mother would lie with her on the bed and share a pillow with her while both would dream of a rose trellis covered with miniature pink roses cascading from one side to the other and pathways bordered with gardenias, irises, blue forget-me knots, daisies, and a mass of other kaleidoscopic colors of floral arrangements. In one section of the garden would be the trickling of a stream of water flowing from the archway surrounding the angel figure in a fountain. Intermittently scattered about the soft grass carpet would be white ornamental iron chairs with pink velvet cushions. The garden would be their haven of escape and no one could bother them there. Like reading, dreams were also methods of escape from a world of harsh reality.

Awakening her from her dream, Wayne hung his head in the nursery doorway to ask what was for supper. Rosie placed the book back in its corner of the cradle. Before she left, she imagined another item in the cradle, but she knew it was just a vision of some type. The handmade cloth doll with its apron of rosettes was reclining elsewhere and Rosie did not have courage at this time to gather it from its secret place. She took one last look at the entire nursery before she exited. She patted her stomach as if to communicate to the babe within that this would be his or her room, a place ready for its new occupant! She would make sure she would prepare her child for the wonders of the world as best she could. She would gather a bouquet of happiness for her child, as she would try also to strew the weeds of trouble and hurt upon the ground to be trampled upon and buried deep within the earth. Rosie knew how despair could stifle someone's life and she had dreams of her child and other future children growing and living full enriched lives–hopefully void of the troubles and worries she encountered while growing up.

Rosie's dreams of having children became alive for her three times as she gave birth to three daughters, Sheila, Brianna, and Meg. She had to undergo several operations to be able to have children and she felt the suffering was well worth the results. With each little girl, Rosie instilled her mother's doctrine of living and learning. She revealed that there are stumbles in life, but with persistence, one can overcome these ruts in life's pathway.

Yet, with life's precious gifts come death's attempts to steal such gifts and Rosie fought hard to keep her second daughter, Brianna, away from the clutch of death as Rosie frantically went from one doctor to another searching for a cure for Brianna's life-threatening respiratory disease. As each doctor would throw his hands in the air and shake his head hopelessly after examining Brianna, Rosie would whisk her away to more doctors and finally after a few visits to specialists at the Medical College of Virginia, Rosie received optimistic news that there were medical means to help Brianna. A mother's instinct told Rosie not to give up hope. God was with her every step of her path. Rosie's combat with Brianna's illness was just one of the many conflicts she faced concerning prolonging a life.

She faced a diseased kidney in which she underwent an operation to have the kidney removed. Her visits to hospitals were rather frequent as she herself had numerous operations concerning her ears, gall bladder, female organs, a knee replacement, and the ever alarming news of diabetes. Rosie remembered her will to live in each venture. She held onto her faith as always. When Wayne faced two open-heart surgeries, though, Rosie placed a tighter rein on her faith. She sought God's help and assurance through each trial of each operation. As she would clasp one hand of Wayne's in the hospital bed, she clasped her Bible in the other. Surrounding the two of them were their three daughters and sons-in-law, and grandchildren. Each family member was united in love; no one could tear apart the family unit. Rie again looked at the tightly wound bird's nest and knew that strength comes from within.

11

The Departure

"Can I take the bird's nest home, please, Rie Rie?" Cliff asked as he again tried to undo the workings of the nest. He pleaded further with his blue eyes that were surrounded by smudges of dirt and clay from his exploring.

"Well, I guess it would be all right. You've seemed to have claimed it already twisting and tugging on it. Just be sure to place it in your bucket and wash your hands once we get home." Rie realized how odd the word "home" sounded as she was standing on the soil of her first home. She heaved herself up from the large rock and as she stood up, she held tightly to her cloth doll and hugged it to her bosom. Her knuckles whitened at the hold she placed on the doll. She came to retrieve it and lay to rest in its place her troubles and worries of her past. Yes, she thought, it was time to return to her present home. She placed her hand on Cliff's shoulder for anchorage while making sure her footing was secure. Glancing around the creek area one more time, she inhaled the last nostalgic air and proceeded to help the boys collect their things for the return trip home. Cliff placed the bird's nest in his bucket along with the rocks, twigs, and other souvenirs of his venture. He smiled up at his grandmother proudly and gratefully for showing him such a fine menagerie of collectibles and sites to remember. Rie brushed whatever loose dirt would fall from Cliff's clothes. She looked at Court to see if he were ready to leave. While she had to peer downward to check on Cliff, she had to raise her eyes upward to see her oldest grandson, Court. He was also wiping his clothes and straightening his posture for the long journey home.

Court knew their mission was successful as he studied his grandmother preparing to walk away from the creek bed. Her white hair seemed untouched by the breeze and debris from the digging they did to locate her doll. She had a peaceful look upon her face as the lines around her blue-green eyes diminished and the only lines apparent on her face were the lines bordering her smile. Her tears were dried; her anguish was gone. Instead of appearing as an inhabitant of this area, she now stood as a visitor who reflected upon a time that was no more—just another dot on a time line that lengthened itself gradually to the future.

Somehow he, too, knew this was her last trip to this place. He was glad he witnessed a part of his grandmother's roots. She was a simple woman, yet she could be quite complex in her various talents. There were still some mysteries he may never know about her, but he did learn several secrets today. He was present to see a part of her former life unravel before him and it only made him marvel and love his grandmother more. Walking with her back in time helped cement his admiration for her. He held out his hand to help steady her through the rough terrain uphill. Surprisingly, she didn't flounder a bit. Her balance was strong and even, as she strode with him and Cliff up the hill toward the lane near the house.

"Did you need to check on anything else here?" Court added as they were walking in the direction home. "Cliff and I will still go with you wherever you need to go."

"No, I have found what I have missed. I feel so happy that I found my doll and that both of you helped me to find it. You boys are my future. I have visited my past and by doing so, I now realize that everything will be all right. What I failed to learn when I was young was that my mother loved me no matter what. I always needed a token or sign or something to confirm my mother loved me. This doll was missing from my life for years and yet, my mother's love remained a constant part of my life, even after her death. I guess this doll is just a symbol of what I had all along!"

Cliff compared his "tokens" to his grandmother's empty tin and cloth doll and he felt he was the victor of today's treasure search. Court held on to his grandmother as he would strike with his shovel at branches and vines leaping at them. The threesome stepped in unison to a slower beat as they passed through the woods along the meandering path. Rie looked for more distinguishing telltale signs of her past as she looked from side to side while walking with Court and Cliff. She didn't look back to the creek bed, though. She knew her journey was onward in the opposite direction now. Just as they had supported coming in to the home place, each grandson held onto his grandmother while leaving the woodland scenery.

As they neared the farmhouse, Rie paused to capture in her mind the scene she now saw. She placed it in her memory beside the scene of the house she remembered from before. She lingered only for a few minutes because the house was being shadowed by the sunset and she knew time was beckoning her to proceed to the lane for more familiar landmarks. Time can certainly play tricks on the mind and for the very few minutes she stood there, she imagined a silhouette of her mother sitting on the front porch. To make the moment more realistic, she could also faintly hear a humming of a hymn in the background. The wind blew instantly and she felt a tingling of cool air around her shoulders. Neither of the boys mentioned any sign of a sound or sight near them, so she knew she was allowing an interlude of her memory to appear. She shuddered a little and turned to face the lane before her.

"Are you all right?" Court asked. "Did you want to go inside the house to look around again?"

"No, all that is there in the house are empty rooms and I prefer restoring my memories of what was once here. This ol' house looks mighty lonely as it stands and I remember it was once full of company. Sometimes the present can be lonelier than the past."

Court and Cliff gave a farewell nod to the bare house protected by the bushes and overgrown weeds. Court wondered how much longer the house would stand. It had endured many years, but Nature would soon claim it as its own when it would dissolve into the earth as a heap of rubble. Court was happy for Rie that it wasn't in this condition yet. As if on cue in a marching band, they all turned toward the lane and began their descent.

The cedar–lined lane provided an escape into another time, another place. They walked slowly not saying a word, but thinking as loud as they could. Cliff imagined telling Gramps of his "treasures' in his bucket. He walked as a soldier returning home from a victorious battle. He let his bucket swing with every impetus of his steps. Satisfied with his "finds," he didn't let his attention sway to any other natural flora while he tried to keep pace with Rie and Court.

Court rested the shovel on his right shoulder as he still held onto Rie. He would glance at her while they walked, waiting for any signs to stop and look or rest. He was glad they had rested at the creek bed, for he would have truly been tired by now if they had walked continuously. The weight of the shovel was trivial compared to the weight of worries on his mind concerning Rie. He still wondered why she chose now of all times to visit her home place and locate her cloth doll. Court was ever conscious of Rie's sixth sense of future happenings and he hoped she was not trying to convey she would be leaving this world any time soon. He knew if she did, though, that she would be in God's Kingdom and Heaven would be a final resting-place, yet he feared her absence in his world on this earth. Court was too attached to Rie to ever entertain the idea of her being gone. It hurt him to think about it. Trying to relieve the pain, he attempted to think of other things as he held onto his grandmother. He finally convinced himself that he was too young and that Rie was too young for any such event to happen. God needed angels here on earth, he convinced himself. He felt Rie slow her pace and he looked at her to discover that she was walking forward, but glancing backward to the straight row of cedar trees they had now passed.

Rie remembered the trees as small twigs and now they were like giants looming over the borders of the lane. Each tree seemed to symbolize events in her life. It's rather funny, but as she was walking, she didn't notice the pattern the trees made. Now, as she was looking back at all the trees together, she could formulate their design better. She thought how this was so much like events in her life. Each happening was for a reason, a part of a design. The trees themselves were planted for several reasons: beauty, shade, protection, and direction. Each event in her life was also planted for several reasons: growth, decisions, realization, and awareness. Just as one tree was useless by itself, so was one event. Together they revealed something as a result. They pointed to or led someone to a conclusion. Rie concluded that she still was learning at the age of sixty-five. She was rather embarrassed to admit that while she felt she had such complicated matters in her life, the solution was always a simple one, as simple as nature. The path was forever in front of her, no matter where she wandered. Even if she detoured to fight reason, she could still at any time, get back on her path. She knew this would be rather ridiculous to tell the boys. They would probably pretend to understand her, not to hurt her feelings, but she knew they would not yet grasp the true meaning of what she wanted to show them. And she also knew that time played a major part in awakenings. Thank God, she still had time.

Remembering the time, she turned full face to the end of the lane and held her grandsons even tighter! Cliff's whole head was smothered in to Rie's chest and he flailed his arms some to give a signal he was suffocating. "I can't breathe, Rie Rie!" he expelled. She then gave released him and held his face in her hands and kissed him gently on his freckled little nose. Cliff was apprehensive that this would lead to more "mushy" affection such as another "bear" hug and more kisses, so he tried to wiggle free to look up at Rie intently to figure what the heck she was doing.

"I love you so much, Clifford!" Rie exclaimed. She still held his face in her hands as she spoke further. "Thank you for coming here with me to help me find a part of myself. I would never know what to do without you and your brother." Cliff didn't know what part of herself was missing and what part she found, but he knew it must have been a serious help he gave for his whole name to be mentioned. He felt as if he just received a citation of some type. He squirmed to free himself while replying, "Sure, Rie Rie. I'm here to help you anytime."

Court saw Rie's attention turn to him and he braced himself for a collision of some type wondering if she were going to tackle him the same way. Instead, as a respect for Court's stature and age, Rie reached up to hug him and placed a kiss on his cheek. "Court, you are my rock, my stronghold. I can depend on you to help me through, too. Thank you for being here for me." Rie's voice faltered some as if she wanted to say more, but she paused and then began walking to the home she has known for the last forty-some years.

Gramps was sitting on the deacon's bench on the front porch when he saw three figures arriving at his driveway. He squinted to see Cliff and Court walking so close to Rie as if to carry her with them down the walkway. Cliff spied Gramps on the porch and he broke away from Rie and Court to run to Gramps to be the first to report today's journey. While running, he took careful measures to make sure the bucket and its contents didn't topple over. He was eager to share with Gramps his prizes! "Gra-a-amps, hey Gra-a-a-amps!" he yelled. "Wait t' ya see what I got!" He rushed upon the porch and gave Gramps a tight hug. "Ya wanna see what's in my bucket?" Cliff exclaimed. "We went on a venture today and I helped Rie Rie find some 'portant things and I found these things in my bucket. Reach in there and hold 'em, Gramps. And there was a creek, Gramps. One 'specially for fishing! And I had to dig 'neath a rock and about two hunerd feet from the rock I chased a butterfly and then I found this nest and I picked these rocks from the ground where there were some worms, too. Court wouldn't let me put the worms in the bucket. Gramps, you shoulda been there. We saw rabbits and birds and I tried looking for a snake in the creek, but I didn't see one. And there was an ol' fort there, too, with some of the windows missing and weeds were around the porch, but I didn't care, 'cause I played in it jus' the same."

Gramps marveled at how many words could come so quickly out of such a little boy. He smiled at Cliff and rubbed his head and peered at the many items in the bucket. "Well, how in the world did you find all these things? You must be a good explorer to hunt these items. You know, you just can't find a bird's nest and slick river rocks like these just anywhere." He chuckled at Cliff's acceptance of the praise he was receiving. "I know one thing, the next time I 'm in my garden and I have trouble looking for my seeds or tools, I'm gonna havta' get you to help me. With your eyes and quick thinking, I can't go wrong. I may need help hauling my garden stuff around, too."

"Oh, Gramps, I can help you! Just call me when you're ready. I may need my spy belt or my army rifle in case of snakes or groundhogs trying to eat vegetables from your garden. I can scare away the crows with my army whistle, too!"

Gramps watched Rie as she came near. Her face was flushed from the lengthy walk, and she had bundled herself against the early evening chill, but she did appear relaxed with a somber facial expression. "Let me help you sit down, Rosie. You need to rest your legs, especially that right knee, remember?" Wayne took his bride's hand and lowered her in to the rocker near the bench on the porch. He waited for her to get her breath to speak. He knew she had undergone many mood changes today with so many memories flooding her mind. He was patient to let her settle herself in. Looking up at Court, who still stood near Rie, Gramps stated, "You and Cliff sit here near Rie and I'll warm up the supper I fixed while y'all were gone. I know y'all are tired and hungry. I sure appreciate you boys escorting your grandmother on her trip. I felt better knowing both of you were with her." With that last remark Gramps vanished inside the house to the kitchen. He moved slower than usual due to Dr. Robinson's stringent advice concerning Gramps's heart.

Rie unfolded herself and stretched in the rocker to let her soles of her shoes scrape the porch floor as she tried to lean over to one corner of the chair using one of the posts as a head rest. She pulled her cloth doll out from under the sweater she wore and she untangled what was left of the yarn that adorned the doll's head. She also examined the doll more carefully now that she knew she had it with her for as long as she wanted it. After making sure the doll was all there, she laid it upon her chest as she rested. She sighed with contentment as she surveyed her home surroundings. " I don't know about the two of you, but I could eat a bear," she said in a hoarse voice.

Cliff said he didn't want to eat a bear, but Gramps's cooking would be just right for him. He could smell the homemade Brunswick stew that was a specialty of Gramps's cooking. Gramps came out of the front door to tell them that the stew would be ready in a few minutes. Court began to anticipate tasting the homegrown vegetables that came right from Gramps's garden. Gramps's way of cleaning out the freezer ended in a delicious stew every time! Gramps suggested to the boys to take their baths while they waited on the stew to heat. Thinking of soaking in a bathtub of nice warm water was very inviting to Court and he excused himself to go first. Bath time wasn't much competition because Cliff would wait until the last minute to go take a bath. It was too much of an ordeal for him.

Cliff poured his bucket contents on the porch floor and he sorted out the various items in groups of his imaginative classifications. Afterwards, he decided to go in the house to get his toy soldiers to use with his newest toys. Gramps sat silently near Rie waiting for her to tell him of her journey. He grabbed her hand and held it while searching her face for any expression of worry. Rie gave him no alarming looks. Instead she placed his hand on her cheek and then she turned and kissed it. "I'm so glad to be here with you, Wayne. For many years, I wondered what it would be like to go to the old home place and I would often dread the thought of journeying there. But, you know, I found it wasn't so bad after all. I had mixed feelings of being scared and curious. I prayed for the strength to help me accept my past."

"Wayne, a past isn't a place or a thing or a person, necessarily. Today, I discovered a past is actually a memory and nothing more. Time can help evaporate any illusions of horrible people, events, or deeds from the past. I felt as if my horrible illusions were puffs of smoke only to appear should I command them to do so. Wayne, there is no reason for me to ever dwell on bad memories, ever! I had to come to grips with my idea that my mother had forsaken me. She never really left me. You know, I sensed her presence today, stronger than before. All these years I wanted her to know I missed her very much. Today, more than any other day, I felt she knew it. By going to the home place I only physically rescued this doll, but mentally I rescued my relationship with my mother. " Wayne felt his hand against Rosie's cheeks become wet from her tears. He knew she needed this release and he reached over to rub her shoulder with his other hand. He didn't have any words for her—just his closeness. They sat together silently but communicating with their touch for the security and understanding they received from each other. Throughout their many years of marriage, Wayne and Rosie complemented each other as comrades against a world that could usher in distress as quickly as harmony.

They broke apart their embrace when they heard Court trying to coerce Cliff to take a bath. They laughed timidly as if they shared a secret and would not get to reveal more of its contents to each other until the boys were in bed. Wayne helped Rosie out of the rocker in to the house. After some old fashioned reasoning, two good-smelling, clean, young grandsons joined their grandparents at the kitchen table bowing their heads in prayer before eating supper. Each held hands and thanked God not only for their daily blessings, but also for the meaning of family love. Rie felt satisfied, not just from the hearty meal she ate, but from a feeling that her life was now complete.

The boys fell asleep earlier than usual and Gramps had to tug at them to get them to go to their beds. They were lounging in the family room and the couch and beanbag chair felt so comfortable. Gramps then turned off the lights and escorted Rie to their bed. She, too, was weary from the trip and he tucked her in, placing the comforter close around her shoulders to keep her warm. He nestled beside her placing his hand above her head brushing her hair with his fingers. Rie was oblivious to his touch because she was beginning to travel in a tunnel that led her to a different place. Gramps noticed she was chilled and he wrapped the comforter tighter around her. Still, Rie was unaware of his touch. She was busy noticing the many beautiful flowers in her secret garden. As she floated about the garden, she heard the light steady stream of water from an angel fountain. She heard a humming on the other side of a rose arbor. There, reposed on a white ornamental garden chair, was her mother singing one of her favorite hymns while arranging a basket of peach-pink roses. On her mother's lap was a worn book that had a faded title. Rie quietly came upon the chair and peaked over her mother's shoulder. She didn't want to disturb her mother. She wanted this image to last and she was afraid she would scare everything away. The book's title was *The Secret Garden.* The flowers were arranged around an object in the center of the basket where lay a handmade rag doll with yellow yarn hair and pink rosettes adorning the lace apron.

About the Author

Marigold Fields lives in Chesterfield County, Virginia, with her husband, two sons, and pet Siberian Husky. She is a fulltime high school English teacher who enjoys creative writing, needlework, reading, travelling, and most of all, spending time with her family!